FOUR
DOLLS

FOUR DOLLS

Rumer Godden

Illustrated by Pauline Baynes

Impunity Jane

The Fairy Doll

The Story of Holly and Ivy

Candy Floss

GREENWILLOW BOOKS

NEW YORK

Library of Congress Cataloging in Publication Data

Godden, Rumer, (date)   Four dolls.
Contents: Impunity Jane — The fairy doll —
The story of Holly and Ivy — [etc.]
1. Dolls — Juvenile fiction.
2. Children's stories, English.
[1. Dolls — Fiction.   2. Short stories]
I. Baynes, Pauline, ill.   II. Title.
PZ7.G54Fo 1984 [E] 83-14157
ISBN 0-688-02801-2

Impunity
Jane

Once there was a little doll who belonged in a pocket. That was what *she* thought. Everyone else thought she belonged in a dolls' house. They put her in one but, as you will see, she ended up in a pocket.

She was four inches high and made of thick china; her arms and legs were joined to her with loops of strong wire; she had painted blue eyes, a red mouth, rosy cheeks, and painted shoes and socks; the shoes were brown, the socks white with blue edges. Her wig of yellow hair was stuck on with strong firm glue. She had no clothes, but written in the middle of her back with a pencil was:

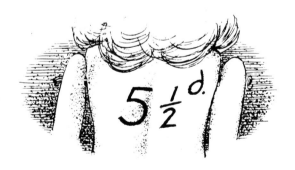

$5\frac{1}{2}d.$

This was in London, England, many years ago, when the streets were lit with gas and boys wore sailor suits and girls had many heavy petticoats. The little doll was in a toy shop. She sat on the counter near a skipping rope, a telescope, and a sailing ship; she was quite at home among these adventurous toys.

Into the toy shop came an old lady and a little girl.

"Grandma?" said the little girl.

"What is it, Effie?" asked the old lady.

"That little doll would just go in my dolls' house!" said Effie.

"But I don't want to go in a dolls' house," said the little doll. "I want to be a skipping rope and dance out into the world, or a sailing ship and go to sea, or a telescope and see the stars!" But she was only a little fivepence-halfpenny doll and in a moment she was sold.

The shop woman was about to wrap her up when the old lady said, "Don't put her in paper. She can go in my pocket."

"Won't she hurt?" said Effie.

"This little doll is very strongly made," said the shop woman. "Why, you could drop her with impunity."

"I know 'imp'," said Effie. "That's a naughty little magic person. But what is impunity?"

"Impunity means escaping without hurt," said the old lady.

7

"That is what I am going to do forever and ever," said the little doll, and she decided that it should be her name. "Imp-imp-impunity," she sang.

Effie called her Jane; afterwards, other children called her Ann or Polly or Belinda, but that did not matter; her name was Impunity Jane.

She went in Grandma's pocket.

Impunity Jane's eyes were so small that she could see through the weave of the pocket. As Effie and Grandma walked home, she saw the bright daylight and sun; she saw trees and grass and the people on the pavements; she saw horses trotting (in those days there were horse buses and carriages, not cars). "Oh, I wish I were a little horse!" cried Impunity Jane.

It was twelve o'clock and the bells were chiming from the church steeples. Impunity Jane heard them, and bicycle bells as well. "Oh, I wish I were a bell!" cried Impunity Jane.

In the park girls and boys were sending shuttlecocks up into the air (in those days children played with shuttlecocks), and Impunity Jane wanted to be a shuttlecock flying up.

In the barracks a soldier was blowing a bugle; it sounded so brave and exciting that it seemed to ring right through her. "A bugle, a horse, a bell, a shuttlecock – oh,

I want to be everything!" cried Impunity Jane.

But she was only a doll; she was taken out of Grandma's pocket, put into Effie's dolls' house, and made to sit on a bead cushion. Have you ever sat on a bead cushion? They are hard and cold, and, to a little doll, the beads are as big as pebbles.

There she sat. "I want to go in a pocket, a pocket, a pocket," wished Impunity Jane, but nobody heard.

Dolls, of course, cannot talk. They can only make wishes that some people can feel.

A dolls' house by itself is just a thing, like a cupboard full of china or a silent musical box; it can live only if it is used and played. Some children are not good at playing; Effie was one. She liked pressing flowers. She did not feel Impunity Jane wishing in the dolls' house.

"I want to go out in a pocket," wished Impunity Jane.

Effie did not feel a thing!

Presently Effie grew up and another child, Elizabeth, had the dolls' house. There were changes in the nursery; the old oil lamp and the candles were taken away, and there was gas light, like that in the streets. Elizabeth's nurse did not wear a high cap, as Effie's nurse had, and Elizabeth's dresses were shorter than Effie's had been; nor did she wear quite so many petticoats.

Elizabeth liked sewing doll's clothes; she made clothes for Impunity Jane, but the stitches, to a little doll, were like carving knives. Elizabeth made a dress and a tiny

muff. The dress was white with blue sprigs, the muff was cotton wool. Impunity Jane would have liked to have worn it as a hat; it could have been like that soldier's cap – and far off she seemed to hear the bugle – but, no, it was a muff. After she was dressed, Elizabeth put her carefully back on the bead cushion.

Through the dolls' house window Impunity Jane could see Elizabeth's brother playing with his clockwork railway under the table; round and round whirred the shining fast train. "Oh! I wish I were a train," said Impunity Jane.

The years went by; Elizabeth grew up and Ethel had the dolls' house. Now the nursery (and the street outside) had electric lights, and there was an electric stove; the old high fender where Effie's and Elizabeth's socks and vests used to dry was taken away. Ethel did not have any petticoats at all, she wore a jersey and skirt and knickers to match.

Ethel liked lessons. She bought a school set with her pocket money, little doll books and a doll blackboard; she taught Impunity Jane reading and writing and arithmetic, and how to draw a thimble and a blackberry and how to sing a scale.

Through the open door Impunity Jane could see Ethel's brother run off down the stairs and take his hoop.

"Do re mi fa so la ti do," sang Ethel.

"Fa! Fa!" said Impunity Jane.

After Ethel there was Ellen, who kept the dolls' house shut.

Ellen wore grey flannel shorts and her curls were tied up in a pony tail. She went to a day school and, if her mother went out in the evening, she had a "sitter".

Ellen was too busy to play; she listened to the radio or stayed for hours in the living room, looking at television.

Impunity Jane had now sat on the bead cushion for more than fifty years. "Take me out," she would wish into Ellen as hard as she could. Impunity Jane nearly cracked with wishing.

Ellen felt nothing at all.

Then one day Ellen's mother said, "Ellen, you had better get out all your toys. Your cousin Gideon is coming to tea."

Ellen pouted and was cross because she did not like boys, and she had to open the dolls' house and dust its furniture and carpets. Everything was thick with dust, even Impunity Jane. She had felt it settling on her, and it made her miserable. The clothes with the big stitches, the lessons, had been better than dust.

"Gideon! Gideon! What a silly name!" said Ellen.

To Impunity Jane it did not sound silly. "G-G-G" – the sound was hard and gay, and she seemed to hear the bugle again, brave and exciting.

Gideon was a boy of seven with brown eyes and curly hair. When he laughed his nose had small wrinkles at the sides, and when he was very pleased – or frightened or ashamed – his cheeks grew red.

From the first moment he came into the nursery he was interested in the dolls' house. "Let me play with it," he said, and he bent down and looked into the rooms.

"You can move the furniture about and put out the cups and saucers, as long as you put them all back," said Ellen.

"*That's* not playing!" said Gideon. "Can't we put the dolls' house up a tree?"

"A tree? Why the birds might nest in it!" said Ellen.

"Do you think they would?" asked Gideon, and he laughed with pleasure. "Think of robins and wrens sitting on the tables and chairs!"

Impunity Jane laughed too.

"Let's put it on a raft and float it on the river," said Gideon.

"Don't be silly," said Ellen. "It might be swept away and go right out to sea."

"Then fishes could come into it," said Gideon.

"Fishes!"

Impunity Jane became excited, but Ellen still said, "No."

Gideon looked at Impunity Jane on the bead cushion. "Does that little doll just sit there doing nothing?" he asked.

"What could she do?" asked Ellen.

Gideon did not answer, but he looked at Impunity Jane with his bright brown eyes; they twinkled, and suddenly Impunity Jane knew she could make Gideon feel. "Rescue me," wished Impunity Jane as hard as she could. "Gideon, rescue me. Don't leave me here, here where Effie and Elizabeth and Ethel and Ellen have kept me so long. Gideon! *Gideon!*"

But Gideon was tired of Ellen and the nursery. "I think I'll take a ball out into the garden," he said.

"Gideon! Gideon, I shall crack!" cried Impunity Jane. "G-I-D-E-O-N! G-I-D-E-O-N!"

Gideon stopped and looked at Impunity Jane; then he looked round at Ellen. Ellen was eating cherries from a plate her mother had brought in; she ought really to have shared them with Gideon, but she had gobbled most of them up; now she was counting the stones. "Tinker, tailor, soldier, sailor," counted Ellen.

"Gideon, Gideon," wished Impunity Jane.

"Rich man, poor man, beggar man" - and just as Ellen said, "Thief", Gideon, his cheeks red, slid his hand into the dolls' house, picked up Impunity Jane, and put her into his pocket.

Ages and ages ago Impunity Jane had been in Grandma's pocket, but Grandma's pocket was nothing to Gideon's. To begin with, Gideon's pockets often had real holes in them, and Impunity Jane could put her head right through them into the world. Sometimes she had to hold onto the edges to avoid falling out altogether, but she was not afraid.

"I'm Imp-imp-impunity," she sang.

Grandma had not run, and oh! the feeling of running, spinning through the air! Grandma had not skated nor ridden on a scooter. "I can skate and I can scoot," said Impunity Jane.

Grandma had not swung; Gideon went on the swings in the park, and Impunity Jane went too, high and higher, high in the air.

Grandma had not climbed trees; Gideon climbed, to the very top, and there he took Impunity Jane out of his pocket and sat her on one of the boughs; she could see far over houses and steeples and trees, and feel the bough moving in the wind.

"I feel the wind. I feel the wind!" cried Impunity Jane.

In Grandma's pocket there had been only Impunity
Jane and a folded white handkerchief that smelled of
lavender water. In Gideon's pockets were all kinds of
things. Impunity Jane never knew what she would find
there – string and corks, sweets and sweet-papers, nuts,
cigarette cards with beautiful pictures, an important
message, a knife with a broken handle, some useful
screws and tacks, a bit of pencil, and, for a long time, a
little brown snail.

The snail had a polished brown shell with smoke-curl

markings. Gideon used to take her out and put her down to eat on the grass; then a head with two horns like a little cow came out at one side of the shell and a small curved tail at the other; the tail left a smeary silvery trail like glue; it made the inside of Gideon's pocket beautifully sticky. Gideon called the snail Ann Rushout because of the slow way she put out her horns.

"I once had a chestnut as a pretend snail," said Gideon, "but a real snail's much better."

Impunity Jane thought so too.

But in all this happiness there was a worry. It worried Gideon, and so, of course, it worried Impunity Jane. (If dolls can make you feel, you make them feel as well.)

The worry was this; Gideon was a boy, and boys do not have dolls, not even in their pockets.

"They would call me 'sissy'," said Gideon, and his cheeks grew red.

On the corner of the street a gang of boys used to meet; they met in the park as well. The leader of the gang was Joe McCallaghan. Joe McCallaghan had brown hair that was stiff as a brush, a turned-up nose, freckles, and grey eyes. He wore a green wolf cub jersey and a belt bristling with knives; he had every kind of knife, and he had bows and arrows, an air gun, a space helmet, and a bicycle with a dual brake control, a lamp, and a bell. He was nine years old and Gideon was only seven but, "He quite likes me," said Gideon.

18

Once Joe McCallaghan pulled a face at Gideon. "Of course, I couldn't *think* of pulling one at him," said Gideon. "He knows me but I can't know him – yet."

Once Gideon had a new catapult, and Joe McCallaghan took it into his hand to look at it. Gideon trembled while Joe McCallaghan stretched the catapult, twanged it, and handed it back. "Decent weapon," said Joe McCallaghan. Gideon would have said "Jolly wizard!" But how ordinary that sounded now! "Decent weapon, decent weapon," said Gideon over and over again.

Impunity Jane heard him and her china seemed to grow cold. Suppose Joe McCallaghan, or one of the gang, should find out what Gideon had in his pocket?

"I should die," said Gideon.

"But I don't look like a proper doll," Impunity Jane tried to say.

That was true. The white dress with the sprigs had been so smeared by Ann Rushout that Gideon had taken it off and thrown it away. Impunity Jane no longer had dresses with stitches like knives; her dresses had no stitches at all. Gideon dressed her in a leaf, or some feathers, or a piece of rag; sometimes he buttoned the rag with a berry. If you can imagine a dirty little gypsy doll, that is how Impunity Jane looked now.

"I'm not a proper doll," she pleaded, but Gideon did not hear.

"Gideon, will you post this letter for me?" his mother asked one afternoon.

Gideon took the letter and ran downstairs and out into the street. Ann Rushout lay curled in her shell, but Impunity Jane put her head out through a brand-new hole. Gideon scuffed up the dust with the toes of his new shoes, and Impunity Jane admired the puffs and the rainbow specks of it in the sun (you look at dust in the sun), and so they came to the postbox.

Gideon stood on tiptoe, and had just posted the letter when – "Hands up!" said Joe McCallaghan. He stepped

out from behind the postbox, and the gang came from
round the corner where they had been hiding.

Gideon was surrounded.

Impunity Jane could feel his heart beating in big jerks.
She felt cold and stiff. Even Ann Rushout woke up and
put out her two little horns.

"Search him," said Joe McCallaghan to a boy called
Puggy.

Impunity Jane slid quickly to the bottom of Gideon's
pocket and lay there under Ann Rushout, the cork, the
sweets, the pencil, and the string.

Puggy ran his hands over Gideon like a policeman and
then searched his pockets. The first thing he found was

Ann Rushout. "A snail. Ugh!" said Puggy and nearly dropped her.

"It's a beautiful snail," said Joe McCallaghan, and the gang looked at Gideon with more respect.

Puggy brought out the cork, the sweets – Joe McCallaghan tried one through the paper with his teeth and handed it back – the pencil, a lucky sixpence, the knife – "Broken," said Puggy scornfully, and Gideon grew red. Puggy brought out the string. Then Impunity Jane felt his fingers close round her, and out she came into the light of day.

Gideon's cheeks had been red; now they went dark, dark crimson. Impunity Jane lay stiffly as Puggy handed her to Joe McCallaghan; the berry she had been wearing broke off and rolled in the gutter.

"A doll!" said Joe McCallaghan in disgust.

"Sissy!" said Puggy. "Sissy!"

"Sissy got a dolly," the gang jeered and waited to see what Joe McCallaghan would do.

"You're a sissy," said Joe McCallaghan to Gideon, as if he were disappointed.

Impunity Jane lay stiffly in his hand. "I'm Imp-imp-impunity," she tried to sing, but no words came.

Then Gideon said something he did not know he could say. He did not know how he thought of it; it might have come out of the air, the sky, the pavement, but amazingly it came out of Gideon himself. "I'm not a sissy," said

Gideon. "She isn't a doll, she's a model. I use her in my model train."

"A model?" said Joe McCallaghan and looked at Impunity Jane again.

"Will he throw me in the gutter like the berry?" thought Impunity Jane. "Will he put me down and tread on me? Break me with his heel?"

"A model," said Gideon firmly.

"She can be a fireman or a porter or a driver or a sailor," he added.

"A sailor?" said Joe McCallaghan, and he looked at Impunity Jane again. "I wonder if she would go in my model yacht," he said. "I had a lead sailor, but he fell overboard."

"She wouldn't fall overboard," said Gideon.

Joe McCallaghan looked at her again. "Mind if I take her to the pond?" he said over his shoulder to Gideon.

Now began such a life for Impunity Jane. She, a little pocket doll, was one of a gang of boys! Because of her, Gideon, her Gideon, was allowed to be in the gang too. "It's only fair," said Joe McCallaghan, whom we can now call Joe, "it's only fair, if we use her, to let him in."

Can you imagine how it feels, if you are a little doll, to sit on the deck of a yacht and go splashing across a pond? You are sent off with a hard push among ducks as big as icebergs, over ripples as big as waves. Most people would have been afraid and fallen overboard, like the lead sailor, but, "Imp-imp-impunity," sang Impunity Jane and reached the far side wet but perfectly safe.

She went up in aeroplanes. Once she was nearly lost when she was tied to a balloon; she might have floated over to France, but Gideon and Joe ran and ran, and at last they caught her in a garden square, where they had to climb the railings and were caught themselves by an old lady, who said she would complain to the police. When they explained that Impunity Jane was being carried off to France, the old lady understood and let them off.

The gang used Impunity Jane for many things: she lived in igloos and wigwams, ranch houses, forts and rocket ships. Once she was put on a Catherine Wheel until Joe thought her hair might catch fire and took her off, but she saw the lovely bright firework go blazing round in a shower of bangs and sparks.

She was with Joe and Gideon when they ran away to sea, and with them when they came back again because it was time for dinner. "Better wait till after Christmas," said Joe. Gideon agreed – he was getting a bicycle for Christmas – but Impunity Jane was sorry; she wanted to see the sea.

Next day she was happy again because they started digging a hole through to Australia, and she wanted to see Australia. When they pretended the hole was a gold mine, she was happy to see the gold, and when the gold mine was a cave and they wanted a fossilized mouse, she was ready to be a fossilized mouse.

"I say, will you sell her?" Joe asked Gideon.

Gideon shook his head, though it made him red to do it. "You can borrow her when you want to," he said: "But she's mine."

But Impunity Jane was not Gideon's; she was Ellen's.

The gang was a very honourable gang. "One finger wet, one finger dry," they said, and drew them across their throats; that meant they would not tell a lie. Gideon knew that even without fingers they would never, never steal, and he, Gideon, had stolen Impunity Jane.

She and Gideon remembered what Ellen had said as she counted cherrystones (do you remember?). "Rich man, poor man, beggar man, thief," said Ellen.

"Thief! Thief!"

Sometimes, to Gideon, Impunity Jane felt as heavy as lead in his pocket; sometimes Impunity Jane felt as heavy and cold as lead herself. "I'm a thief!" said Gideon and grew red.

Impunity Jane could not bear Gideon to be unhappy. All night she lay awake in his pyjama pocket. "What shall I do?" asked Impunity Jane. She asked Ann Rushout. Ann Rushout said nothing, but in the end the answer came. Perhaps it came out of the night, or Ann's shell, or out of Gideon's pocket, or even out of Impunity Jane herself. The answer was very cruel. It said, "You must

wish Gideon to put you back."

"Back? In the dolls' house?" said Impunity Jane. "Back, with Ellen, Ellen who kept it shut?" And she said slowly, "Ellen was worse than Ethel or Elizabeth or Effie. I can't go back," said Impunity Jane, "I can't!" But, from far off, she seemed to hear the bugle telling her to be brave, and she knew she must wish, "Gideon, put me back."

She wanted to say, "Gideon, hold me tightly," but she said, "Gideon, put me back."

So Gideon went back to Ellen's house with Impunity Jane in his pocket. He meant to edge round the nursery door while his mother talked to Ellen's mother, then open the dolls' house and slip Impunity Jane inside and onto the bead cushion. He went upstairs, opened the nursery door, and took Impunity Jane in his hand.

It was the last minute. "No more pockets," said Impunity Jane. "No more running and skating and swinging in the air. No more igloos and ripples. No rags and berries for frocks. No more Ann Rushout. No more warm dirty fingers. No more feeling the wind. No more Joe, no gang, not even Puggy. No more . . . Gideon!" cried Impunity Jane – and she cracked.

But what was happening in Ellen's nursery? The dolls' house was not in its place – it was on the table with a great many other toys, and there was Ellen sorting them and doing them up in parcels.

"I'm going to give all my toys away," said Ellen with

a toss of her head. "I'm too old to play with them any more. I'm going to boarding school. Wouldn't you like to go to boarding school?" she said to Gideon.

"No," said Gideon.

"Of course, you're still a *little* boy," said Ellen. "You still like toys."

"Yes," said Gideon, and his fingers tightened on Impunity Jane.

"Would you like a toy?" asked Ellen, who was polishing a musical box.

"Yes," said Gideon.

"What would you like?" asked Ellen.

"Please," said Gideon. His cheeks were bright red. "Please" – and he gulped – "could I have" – gulp – "the pocket doll" – gulp – "from the dolls' house?"

"Take her," said Ellen without looking up.

Gideon has a bicycle now. Impunity Jane rides on it with him. Sometimes she is tied to the handlebars, but sometimes Gideon keeps her where she likes to be best of all, in his pocket. Now Impunity Jane is not only his model, she is his mascot, which means she brings him luck.

The crack was mended with china cement by Gideon's mother.

Ellen went to boarding school.

As for the dolls' house, it was given away.

As for the bead cushion, it was lost.

The Fairy
Doll

Nobody knew where she came from.

"She must have belonged to Mother when Mother was a little girl," said Father, but Mother did not remember it.

"She must have come from Father's house, with the Christmas decorations," said Mother, but Father did not remember it.

As long as the children could remember, at Christmas every year, the fairy doll had been there at the top of the Christmas tree.

She was six inches high and dressed in a white gauze dress with beads that sparkled; she had silver wings, and a narrow silver crown on her dark hair, with a glass dewdrop in front that sparkled too; in one of her hands she had a silver wand, and on her feet were silver shoes – not painted, stitched. "Fairies must have sewn those," said Mother.

"Or mice," said Christabel, who was the eldest.

Elizabeth, the youngest, was examining the stitches. "Fairy mice," said Elizabeth.

You may think it is a lucky thing to be the youngest, but for Elizabeth it was not lucky at all; she was told what to do – or what not to do – by her sisters and brother all day long, and she was always being left out or made to stay behind.

"You can't come, you're too young," said Christabel.

"You can't reach. You're too small," said Godfrey, who was the only boy.

"You can't play. You're too little," said Josie. Josie was only two years older than Elizabeth, but she ordered her about most of all.

Christabel was eight, Godfrey was seven, Josie was six, but Elizabeth was only four and she was different from the others: they were thin, she was fat; their legs were long, hers were short; their hair was curly, hers was straight; their eyes were blue, hers were grey and easily filled with tears. They rode bicycles; Christabel's was green, Godfrey's red, Josie's dark blue. Elizabeth rode the old tricycle; its paint had come off, and its wheels went "Wh-ee-ze, wh-ee-ze, wh-ee-ze."

"Slowpoke," said Christabel, whizzing past.

"Tortoise," said Godfrey.

"Baby," said Josie.

"Not a slowpoke, tortoise, baby," said Elizabeth, but they did not hear; they were far away, spinning down the hill. "Wh-ee-ze, wh-ee-ze, wh-ee-ze," went the tricycle, and Elizabeth's eyes filled with tears.

"Cry-baby," said Josie, who had come pedalling back, and the tears spilled over. Then that Christmas, Elizabeth saw the fairy doll.

She had seen her before, of course, but, "Not really,"

said Elizabeth; not properly – as you shall hear.

Every year there were wonderful things on the Christmas tree: tinsel and icicles of frosted glass that had been Father's when he was a little boy: witch balls in colours like jewels and a trumpet of golden glass – it had been father's as well – and bells that were glass too but coloured silver and red. Have you ever rung a glass bell? Its clapper gives out a "ting" that is like the clearest, smallest, sweetest voice.

There were silvered nuts and little net stockings filled with gold and silver coins. Can you guess what the coins were? They were chocolate. There were transparent boxes of rose petals and violets and mimosa. Can you guess what they were? They were sweets. There were Christmas crackers and coloured lights and candles.

When the lights were lit, they shone in the dewdrop on the fairy doll's crown, making a bead of light; it twinkled when anybody walked across the room or touched the tree, and the wand stirred in the fairy doll's hand. "She's alive!" said Elizabeth.

"Don't be silly," said Christabel, and she said scornfully, "*What* a little silly you are!"

Thwack. A hard small box of sweets fell off the tree and hit Christabel on the head.

The fairy doll looked straight in front of her, but the wand stirred gently, very gently, in her hand.

In the children's house, on the landing, was a big chest

carved of cedar wood; blankets were stored in it and spare clothes. The Christmas things were kept there too; the candles had burned down, of course, and the crackers had been snapped and the sweets and nuts eaten up, but after Christmas everything else was packed away; last of all the fairy doll was wrapped in blue tissue paper, put in a cotton-reel box, laid with the rest in the cedar chest, and the lid was shut.

When it was shut, the chest was still useful. Mother sent the children to sit on it when they were naughty. The next Christmas Elizabeth was five. "You can help to dress the tree," said Mother and gave her some crackers to tie on. "Put them on the bottom branches, and then people can pull them," said Mother.

The crackers were doll-size, silver, with silver fringes; they were so pretty that Elizabeth did not want them pulled; she could not bear to think of them tattered and torn, and she hid them in the moss at the bottom of the tree.

"*What* are you doing?" said Godfrey in a terrible voice.

He had been kneeling on the floor with his stamp collection, for which he had a new valuable purple British Guiana stamp. He jumped up and jerked the crackers out.

"You're afraid of the bang so you hid them," he said.

Elizabeth began to stammer "I – I wasn't –" But he was already jumping round her, singing, "Cowardy,

cowardy custard."

"Cowardy, cowardy custard . . ."

A gust of wind came under the door; it lifted up the new valuable purple British Guiana stamp and blew it into the fire.

The fairy doll looked straight in front of her, but the wand stirred gently, very gently, in her hand.

Elizabeth was often naughty; she did not seem able to help it, and that year she spent a great deal of time sitting on the cedar chest.

As she sat, she would think down through the cedar wood, and the cotton-reel box, and the blue tissue paper, to the fairy doll inside.

Then she did not feel quite as miserable.

The Christmas after that she was six; she was allowed to tie the witch balls and the icicles on the tree but not to touch the trumpet or the bells. "But I can help to light the candles, can't I?" asked Elizabeth.

Josie had been blowing up a balloon; it was a green balloon she had bought with her own money, and she had blown it to a bubble of emerald. You must have blown up balloons, so you will know what hard work it is. Now Josie took her lips away for a moment and held the balloon carefully with her finger and thumb.

"Light the candles!" she said to Elizabeth. "You?

You're far too young."

Bang went the balloon.

The fairy doll looked straight in front of her, but the wand stirred gently, very gently, in her hand.

Under the tree was a small pale blue bicycle, shining with paint and steel; it had a label that read: ELIZABETH.

"You lucky girl," said Mother.

The old tricycle was given to a children's home; it would never go "wh-ee-ze, wh-ee-ze" for Elizabeth again. She took the new bicycle and wheeled it carefully onto the road. "You lucky girl," said everyone who passed.

Elizabeth rang the bell and once or twice she put her foot on the pedal and took it off again. Then she wheeled the bicycle home.

That year Elizabeth was naughtier than ever and seemed able to help it less and less.

She spilled milk on the Sunday newspapers before Father had read them; she broke Mother's Wedgwood

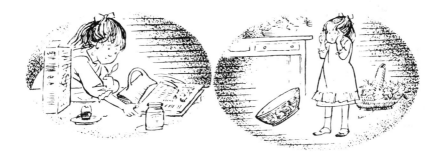

bowl, and by mistake she mixed the paints in Christabel's new paintbox. "Careless little idiot," said Christabel. "I told you not to touch."

When Mother sent Elizabeth to the shop she forgot matches or flour or marmalade, and Godfrey had to go and get them. "You're a perfect duffer," said Godfrey, furious. Going to dancing, she dropped the penny for her bus fare, and Josie had to get off the bus with her.

"I'll never forgive you. Never," said Josie.

It grew worse and worse. Every morning when they were setting off to school, "Elizabeth, you haven't brushed your teeth," Christabel would say, and they had to wait while Elizabeth went back. Then they scolded her all the way to school.

At school it was no better. She seemed more silly and stupid every day. She could not say her tables, especially the seven-times; she could not keep up in reading, and

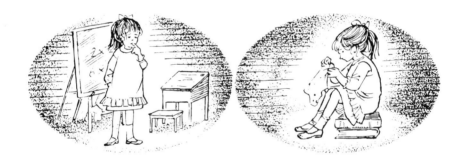

when she sewed, she pricked her finger so much that the cloth had blood stains.

"Oh, Elizabeth, why are you such a stupid child?" asked Miss Thrupp, the teacher.

Sometimes, that year, Elizabeth got down behind the cedar chest, though it was dusty there, and lay on the floor. "I wish it was Christmas," she said to the fairy doll inside. Then she would remember something else and say, "I wish it never had been Christmas," because, worst of all, Elizabeth could not learn to ride her bicycle.

Father taught her, and Mother taught her; Christabel never stopped teaching her. "Push, pedal; pedal pedal pedal," cried Christabel, but Elizabeth's legs were too short.

"Watch me," said Godfrey, "and you won't wobble." But Elizabeth wobbled.

"Go fast," said Josie. "Then you won't fall." But Elizabeth fell.

All January, February, March, April, May, and June she tried to ride the bicycle. In July and August they went to the sea so that she had a little rest; in September, October, November she tried again, but when December came, Elizabeth still could not ride the bicycle.

"And you're seven years old!" said Christabel.

"More like seven months!" said Godfrey.

"Baby! Baby!" said Josie.

Great-Grandmother was to come that year for Christmas. None of the children had seen her before because she had been living in Canada. "Where's Canada?" asked Elizabeth.

"Be quiet," said Christabel.

Great-Grandmother was Mother's mother's mother. "And very old," said Mother.

"How old?" asked Elizabeth.

"Ssh," said Godfrey.

There was to be a surprise; the children were to march

into the drawing room and sing a carol, and when the carol was ended Great-Grandmother was to be given a basket of roses. But the basket was not a plain basket; it was made, Mother told them, of crystal.

"What's crystal?" asked Elizabeth.

"Shut up," said Josie, but, "It's the very finest glass," said Mother.

The roses were not plain roses either; they were Christmas roses, snow-white. Elizabeth had expected them to be scarlet. "*Isn't* she silly?" said Josie.

Who was to carry the basket? Who was to give it? "I'm the eldest," said Christabel. "It ought to be me."

"I'm the boy," said Godfrey. "It ought to be me."

"I'm Josephine after Great-Grandmother," said Josie. "It ought to be me."

"Who is to give it? Who?" In the end they asked Mother, and Mother said, "Elizabeth."

"*Elizabeth?*"

"*Elizabeth?*"

"*Elizabeth?*"

"Why?" They all wanted to know.

"Because she's the youngest," said Mother.

None of them had heard that as a reason before, and –

"It's too heavy for her," said Christabel.

"She'll drop it," said Godfrey.

"You know what she is," said Josie.

"I'll be very, very careful," said Elizabeth.

How proud she was when Mother gave the handsome, shining basket into her hands outside the drawing room door! It was so heavy that her arms ached, but she would not have given it up for anything in the world. Her heart beat under her velvet dress, her cheeks were red, as they marched in and stood in a row before Great-Grandmother. "Noel, Noel," they sang.

Great-Grandmother was sitting in the armchair; she had a white shawl over her knees and a white scarf patterned with silver over her shoulders; to Elizabeth she looked as if she were dressed in white and silver all over; she even had white hair, and in one hand she held a thin stick with a silver top. She had something else, and Elizabeth stopped in the middle of a note; at the end of Great-Grandmother's nose hung a dewdrop.

An older, cleverer child might have thought, Why doesn't Great-Grandmother blow her nose? But to Elizabeth that trembling, shining drop was beautiful; it caught the shine from the Christmas tree and, if Great-Grandmother moved, it twinkled; it reminded Elizabeth of something, she could not think what. She gazed so hard that she did not hear the carol end.

". . . Born is the King of Is-ra-el."

There was a silence.

"Eliza*beth!*" hissed Christabel.

"Go *on*," whispered Godfrey.

Josie gave Elizabeth a push.

Elizabeth jumped and dropped the basket.

The Christmas roses were scattered on the carpet and the crystal basket was broken to bits.

Hours afterward – it was really one hour, but to Elizabeth it felt like hours – Mother came upstairs. "Great-Grandmother wants to see you," she said.

Elizabeth was down behind the chest. The velvet dress was dusty now, but she did not care. She had not come out to have tea nor to see her presents. "What's the use of giving Elizabeth presents?" she had heard Father say.

"She doesn't ride the one she has."

Elizabeth had made herself flatter and flatter behind the cedar chest; now she raised her head. "Great-Grandmother *wants* to see me?" she asked.

Great-Grandmother looked at Elizabeth, at her face, which was red and swollen with tears, at her hands that had dropped the basket, at her legs that were too short to ride the bicycle, at her dusty dress.

"H'm," said a voice. "Something will have to be done."

It must have been Great-Grandmother's voice, there was nobody else in the room; but it seemed to come from high up, a long way up, from the top of the tree, for instance; at the same moment there was a swishing sound as of something brushing through branches, wings perhaps, and the fairy doll came flying – it was falling, of course, but it sounded like flying – down from the tree to the carpet. She landed by Great-Grandmother's stick.

"Dear me! How fortunate," said Great-Grandmother, and now her voice certainly came from her. "I was just going to say you needed a good fairy."

"Me?" asked Elizabeth.

"You," said Great-Grandmother. "You had better have this one."

Elizabeth looked at the fairy doll, and the fairy doll looked at Elizabeth; the wand was still stirring with the rush of the fall.

"What about the others?" asked Elizabeth.

"You can leave the others to me," said Great-Grandmother.

"What about next Christmas and the tree?"

"Next Christmas is a long way off," said Great-Grandmother. "We'll wait and see."

Slowly Elizabeth knelt down on the floor and picked up the fairy doll.

"How can I take care of her?" asked Elizabeth.

"She is to take care of you," said Mother, but fairies have a way of doing things the wrong way round.

"Pooh! She's only an ordinary doll dressed up in fairy clothes," said Josie, who was jealous.

"She's not ordinary," said Elizabeth, and, as you will see, Elizabeth was right.

"What's her name?" asked Josie.

"She doesn't need a name. She's Fairy Doll," said Elizabeth, and, "How dare I take care of her?" she asked.

Fairy Doll looked straight in front of her, but Elizabeth must have touched the wand; it stirred gently, very gently, in Fairy Doll's hand.

"Where will she live?" asked Josie. "She can't live in the dolls' house. Fairies don't live anywhere," said Josie scornfully.

"They must," said Elizabeth. "Mother says some people think fairies were the first people, so they must have lived somewhere." And she went and asked Father, "Father, where did the first people live?"

"In caves, I expect," said Father.

"Elizabeth can't make a cave," said Josie.

Elizabeth had just opened her mouth to say, "No," when "Ting" went a sound in her head. It was as clear and small as one of the glass Christmas bells.

"Ting. Bicycle basket," it said.

Elizabeth knew what a cave was like; there had been caves at the seaside; there was one in the big wood across the field, and this very Christmas there was a clay model cave, in the Crèche, at school. If she had been a clever child she would have argued, "Bicycle basket? Not a bicycle basket?" but, not being clever, she went to look. She unstrapped the basket from her bicycle and put it on its side.

The "ting" had been right; the bicycle basket, on its side, was exactly the shape of a cave.

The cave in the wood had grass on its top, brambles and bracken and trees and grass. "What's fairy grass?" asked Elizabeth, and "Ting", a word rang in her head. The word was "moss".

She knew where moss was; they had gathered some from the wood for the Christmas-tree tub. A week ago Elizabeth would not have gone to the wood alone, but now she had Fairy Doll and she set out through the garden, across the road and fields; soon she was back with her skirt held up full of moss.

She covered the outside of the bicycle basket with the moss like a cosy green thatch; then she stood the basket on a box and made a moss lawn around it. "Later on I'll have beds of tiny real flowers," she said.

It is odd how quickly you get used to things; Elizabeth asked, and the "ting" answered; it was a little like a slot machine. "What shall I put on the floor?" she asked.

"Ting. In the garage."

A cleverer child would have said, "In the *garage?*" Josie, for instance, would not have gone there at all, but Elizabeth went, and there, in the garage, Father was sawing up logs.

"What did they put on the cave floors?" asked Elizabeth.

"Sand, I expect," said Father.

Sand was far, far away at the seaside; Elizabeth was just going to say, with a sigh, that that was no good when she looked at the pile of sawdust that had fallen from the logs, and, "Sawdust! Fairy sand," said the "ting".

"What about a bed?" said Josie.

"A bed?" asked Elizabeth, and back came the "ting". "Try a shell."

"A coconut shell?" asked Elizabeth, watching the blue tits swinging on the bird table, but a coconut seemed coarse and rough for a little fairy doll. A shell? A shell? Why not a real shell? Elizabeth had brought one back from the seaside; she had not picked it up, the landlady had given it to her; it was big, deep pink inside, and if you held it to your ear you heard, far off, the sound of the sea; it sounded like a lullaby. Fairy Doll could lie in the shell and listen; it made a little private radio.

The shell needed a mattress. "Flowers," said the "ting".

Josie would have answered that there were no flowers now, but, "Is there a soft winter flower, like feathers?" asked Elizabeth. "Ting" came the answer. "Old man's beard."

Do you know old man's beard that hangs on the trees

and the hedges from autumn to winter? Its seeds hang in a soft fluff, and Elizabeth picked a handful of it; then she found a deep red leaf for a cover; it was from the Virginia creeper that grew up the front of the house.

Soon the cave was finished – "and with fairy things," said Elizabeth. She asked Father to cut her two bits from a round, smooth branch; they were three inches high and made a table and a writing desk. There were toadstools for stools; stuck in the sawdust, they stood upright. On the table were acorn cups and bowls, and small leaf plates. Over the writing desk was a piece of dried-out honeycomb; it was exactly like the rack of pigeonholes over Father's desk. Fairy Doll could keep her letters there, and she could write letters; Elizabeth found a tiny feather and asked Godfrey to cut its point to make a quill pen like the one Mother had, and for writing paper there were petals of a Christmas rose. If you scratch a petal with a pen, or, better still, a pin, it makes fairy marks. "Later on there'll be all sorts of flower writing-paper," said Elizabeth.

There was a broom made of a fir-twig, a burr for a door-scraper; a berry on a thread made a knocker. "In summer I'll get you a dandelion clock," she told Fairy Doll.

"You haven't got a bath," said Josie.

"Fairies don't need baths," said Elizabeth. "They wash outside in the dew."

It was odd; she was beginning to know about fairies.

"What does she eat?" asked Josie.

"Snow ice-cream," said Elizabeth – it was snowing – "holly baked apples, and the hips off the rose trees."

"Hips are too big for a little doll like that," said Josie.

"They are fairy pineapples," said Elizabeth with dignity.

"Look what Elizabeth has made," cried Christabel, and she said in surprise, "It's pretty!"

Godfrey came to look. "Gosh!" said Godfrey.

Josie put out her hand to touch a toadstool, and a funny feeling stirred inside Elizabeth, a feeling like a hard little wand.

"Don't touch," said Elizabeth to Josie.

Spring came, and Fairy Doll had a hat made out of a crocus, and a pussywillow-fuzz powder puff; she ate fairy bananas, which were bunches of catkins – rather large bananas – and fairy lettuces, which were hawthorn buds – rather small; she ate French rolls, the gold-brown beech-leaf buds, with primrose butter; the beds in the moss lawn were planted with violets out of the wood.

One morning, as they were all starting off to school, Christabel said, as usual, "Elizabeth, you haven't brushed your teeth."

Elizabeth was going back when she stopped. "But I have," she said. She had been in the bathroom, and

"Ting. Brush your teeth" had come in her head. "I've brushed them," said Elizabeth, amazed. Christabel was amazed as well.

A few days afterwards Miss Thrupp said in school, "Let's see what Elizabeth can do," which meant "Let's see what Elizabeth can't do."

"Stand up, Elizabeth, and say the seven-times table."

"Seven times one are seven," said Elizabeth, and there was a long, long pause.

"Seven times two?" Miss Thrupp said encouragingly.

Elizabeth stood dumb, and the class began to laugh.

"Hush, children. Seven times two . . ."

"Ting. Are fourteen." And Elizabeth went on. "Seven threes are twenty-one, seven fours are twenty-eight . . ." right up to "Seven twelves are eighty-four."

At the end Miss Thrupp and the children were staring. Then they clapped.

In reading they had come to "The Sto-ry of the Sleep-ing Beau-ty." Elizabeth looked hopelessly at all the difficult words; her eyes were just beginning to fill with tears when, "Ting", the words "Li-lac Fai-ry" seemed to skip off the page into her head. "It says 'Lilac Fairy,'" she said.

"Go on," said Miss Thrupp, "go on," and Elizabeth went on. " 'Li-lac Fai-ry. Spin-ning Wheel. Prince Charm-ing.' "

"Ting. Ting. Ting" went the bell.

"Good girl, those are difficult words!" said Miss Thrupp.

In sewing they began tray-cloths in embroidery stitches; perhaps it was from making the small-sized fairy things that Elizabeth's fingers had learned to be neat; the needle went in and out, plock, plock, plock, and there was not a trace of blood. "You're getting quite nimble," said Miss Thrupp, and she told the class, "Nimble means clever and quick."

"Does she mean I'm *clever*?" Elizabeth asked the little boy next to her. She could not believe it.

Soon it was summer. Fairy Doll had a Canterbury bell for a hat; her bed had a peony-petal cover now. She ate daisy poached eggs, rose-petal ham, and lavender rissoles. Lady's slipper and pimpernels were planted in the moss.

"What's the matter with Elizabeth?" asked Godfrey. "She's not half such a little duffer as she was."

That was true. She was allowed to take the Sunday newspapers in for Father, and Mother trusted her to wash up by herself.

"You can use my paintbox if you like," said Christabel.

"You can take your own bus money," said Josie.

"Run to the shop," said Mother, "and get me a mop and a packet of matches, a pot of strawberry jam, half a pound of butter, and a pound of ginger nuts."

"What have you brought?" she asked when Elizabeth came back.

"A pound of ginger nuts, half a pound of butter, a pot of strawberry jam, a packet of matches, and a mop," said Elizabeth, counting them out.

"But you still can't ride the bicycle," said Josie.

It grew hot, Fairy Doll had a nasturtium leaf for a sun-shade, and Elizabeth made her a poppy doll. To make a poppy doll you turn the petals back and tie them down with a grass blade for a sash; the middle of the poppy makes the head, with the fuzz for hair, and for arms you take a bit of poppy stalk and thread it through under the petals; then the poppy doll is complete, except that it has only one leg. Perhaps that was why Fairy Doll did not play with hers.

Something was the matter with Fairy Doll; her dress had become a little draggled and dirty after all these months, but it was more than that; her wings looked limp, the wand in her hand was still. Something was the matter in Elizabeth too; the bell did not say "Ting" any more in her head. "Dull, Dull, Dull," it said.

"Dull?" asked Elizabeth.

"Dull, Dull, Dull." It was more like a drum than a bell.

"Does it mean Fairy Doll is dull with me?" asked Elizabeth.

She felt sad; then she felt ashamed.

A fairy likes flying. Naturally. If you had wings you would like flying too. Sometimes Elizabeth would hold Fairy Doll up in the air and run with her; then the wings would lift, the wand would wave, the gauze dress fly back, but Elizabeth was too plump to run for long.

"I'll put her on my bicycle and fly her," Godfrey offered.

"You mustn't touch her," cried Elizabeth.

"Well, fly her yourself," said Godfrey, offended, and he rode off.

"Fly her yourself." "Ting" went the bell, and it was a bell, not a drum. "Ting. Ting. Fly. Fly." So that was what Fairy Doll was wishing! Elizabeth went slowly into the garage and looked at the pale blue, still brand-new bicycle.

"It doesn't hurt so much to fall off in summer as in winter," said Elizabeth, but her voice trembled. Her fingers trembled too, as she tied Fairy Doll onto the handlebars.

Then Elizabeth put her foot on the pedal. "Push. Pedal, pedal," she said and shut her eyes, but you cannot ride even the smallest bicycle with your eyes shut.

She had to open them, but it was too late to stop. The drive from the garage led down a slope to the gate, and "Ting", away went the bicycle with Elizabeth on it. For a moment she wobbled; then she saw the silver wings filling and thrilling as they rushed through the air, and the

wand blew round and round. "Pedal. Pedal, pedal." It might have been Christabel talking, but it was not. "Pedal." Elizabeth's hair was blown back, the wind rushed past her, she felt she was flying too; she came to the gate and fell off. "Ow!" groaned Elizabeth, but she had flown. She knew what Fairy Doll wanted. Her leg was bleeding, but she turned the bicycle round to start off down the drive again.

Elizabeth was late for tea.

"What *have* you been doing?" asked Christabel. "There's no jam left." But Elizabeth did not care.

"You've torn your frock. All the buns are gone," said Godfrey, but Elizabeth did not care.

"You're all over scratches and dust," said Josie. "We've eaten the cake." But Elizabeth still did not care.

"Well, where have you been?" asked Mother.

Elizabeth answered, "Riding my bicycle."

Christabel was pleased. Godfrey was very pleased, but Josie said, "Pooh! It isn't Elizabeth who does things, it's Fairy Doll."

"Is it?" asked Elizabeth.

"Try without her and you'll see," said Josie.

Elizabeth looked at Fairy Doll, who was sitting by her on the table. "But I'm not without her," said Elizabeth.

Autumn came and brought the fruit; briony berries were fairy plums and greengages; a single blackberry pip was a grape. A hazel nut was pork with crackling. In every garden people were making bonfires, and Elizabeth made one in the fairy garden; it was of pine needles and twigs, and she watched it carefully; its smoke went up no bigger than a feather. It was altogether a fairy time. In the wood she found toadstools so close together that they looked like chairs put ready for a concert; she gave a fairy concert, but, "It ought to be crickets and nightingales," said Elizabeth. There were silver trails over the leaves and grass. "Fairy paths," she said.

"Snails," snapped Josie. No doubt about it, Josie was jealous.

School began, and Elizabeth was moved up; she was learning the twelve-times table, reading to herself, and knitting a scarf. She was allowed to ride her bicycle on the main road, and to stay up till half-past seven every night.

Then, on a late October day when the first frost was on the grass, Fairy Doll was lost.

"You must have dropped her on the road," said Mother.

"But I didn't."

"Perhaps you left her at school."

"I didn't."

"In your satchel." "In your pocket . . ." "On the counter in the shop." "In the bathroom." "On the book-shelf." "Behind the clock." "Up in the apple tree."

"I didn't. I didn't. I didn't," sobbed Elizabeth.

Everyone was very kind. They all looked everywhere, high and low, up and down, in and out. Godfrey said he looked under every leaf in the whole garden that was big enough. It was no good. Fairy Doll was lost.

Elizabeth went and lay down on the floor behind the cedar chest; she only came out to have a cup of milk and go to bed.

Next morning she went behind the chest and lay down again.

"Make her come out," said Josie, who seemed curiously worried.

"Leave her alone," said Mother.

"She must come out. She has to go to school." But Elizabeth would not go to school. How could she? She could not say her tables now, or spell or read or sew, and she had not brushed her teeth. The tears made a wet place in the dust on the floor. "And I can't ride my bicycle," she said.

It was Christabel's birthday. Christabel was twelve. Elizabeth had a present done up in yellow paper; it was a peppermint lollipop, but she did not give it to Christabel.

She stayed most of the day behind the cedar chest, and a day can feel like weeks when you are seven years old.

"Make her come out," said Josie.

At four o'clock Mother came up. "Great-Grandmother has come for the birthday tea," she said.

"Great-Grandmother?" Elizabeth lay very still.

"I should come down if I were you," said Mother.

Last time Great-Grandmother came she had sent for Elizabeth and Elizabeth had come with a tearstained face. It was tearstained now, but, "I could wash it," said Elizabeth and from somewhere she thought she heard a "Ting". Her dress had been dirty; it was dirty now, but, "I could change it," said Elizabeth, and she heard another "Ting". It was faint and faraway; it could not have been a "Ting" because the chest was empty, the fairy doll was gone, but it sounded like a "Ting". Very slowly Elizabeth sat up.

"Good afternoon, Elizabeth," said Great Grandmother. No one else took any notice as Elizabeth, brushed and clean, in a clean dress, put the present by Christabel and slid into her own place.

She was stiff from lying on the floor, her head ached and her throat was sore from crying, and she was hungry.

Mother gave her a cup of tea; the tea was sweet and hot, and there were minced chicken sandwiches with lettuce, shortcake biscuits, chocolate tarts, sponge fingers, and meringues, besides the birthday cake. Mother passed the sandwiches to Elizabeth and gave her another cup of tea. Elizabeth began to feel much better.

Christabel's cake was pink and white. It had CHRISTABEL, HAPPY BIRTHDAY written on it, and twelve candles.

"And I," said Great-Grandmother, "am eight times twelve." A dewdrop slid down her nose and twinkled. "Eight times twelve. Who can tell me what that is?" asked Great-Grandmother.

With her eyes on the dewdrop, before any of the others could answer – "Ting. Ninety-six," said Elizabeth.

After tea they had races. One was The Button, the Thread, and the Needle. "I can race that," said Great-Grandmother. "I'll have Elizabeth for my partner."

Great-Grandmother threaded the needle as she sat in a chair. Elizabeth had to run with the button, sew it to a patch of cloth, and run back. "I can't . . ." she began, but,

"Nimble fingers," said Great-Grandmother; the stitches flew in and out, the button was on, Elizabeth ran back, and she and Great-Grandmother won the double prize, magic pencils that wrote in four colours.

"Dear me, how annoying!" said Great-Grandmother. "I had meant to stop at the shop and get a few things – some silver polish, a packet of Lux, a one-and-sixpenny duster, and a nutmeg – and I forgot. Elizabeth, hop on your bicycle and get them for me."

"But I can't . . ."

"Here's five shillings," said Great-Grandmother. "Bring me the change."

"Ting". Before Elizabeth knew where she was, she was out on the road, riding her bicycle and perfectly steady. Soon she was back with all the things and one-and-fourpence change for Great-Grandmother.

"Then were the 'tings' me?" asked Elizabeth, puzzled. She could not believe it. "I thought they were Fairy Doll."

"I thought so too," said Josie. She sounded disappointed.

"How could they be?" asked Godfrey.

"They couldn't," said Christabel, who after all was twelve now and ought to know. "Don't be silly," said Christabel. "She was just a doll."

"*Fairy* Doll." It was Great-Grandmother who corrected Christabel, but her voice sounded high up and far away – As if it came from somewhere else? asked Elizabeth.

In the country, November and December are the best times for hedges, but now no one picked the old man's beard for a mattress, or winter berries to bake; no one went to the wood for fresh moss and new toadstools. The fairy house was broken up; the bicycle basket was on the bicycle.

For Christmas they each chose what they would get.

"A writing case," said Christabel.

"A reversing engine, Number Fifty-one, for my Hornby trains," said Godfrey.

"A kitchen set," said Josie.

Elizabeth did not know what she wanted. "Another fairy doll?" suggested Christabel.

"Another! There isn't another," said Elizabeth, shocked. "She was Fairy Doll."

On Christmas Eve the tree was set up in the drawing room. Mother opened the cedar chest and brought the decorations down, the tinsel and the icicles, the witch balls and trumpets and bells, the lights and candle clips. There were new candles, new boxes of sweets, new little bags of nuts, shining new coins, and new crackers. "But what shall we put at the top?" asked Christabel.

Elizabeth ran out of the room, upstairs to the cedar

chest.

She was going to cast herself down – "and stay there; I don't want Christmas," said Elizabeth – but the lid of the chest was open, and, on top of a pile of blankets and folded summer vests, she saw the cotton-reel box that had held Fairy Doll.

"Empty," said Elizabeth. "Empty."

She was just beginning to sob when, "Look in the box," went a loud, clear "ting". "Look in the box."

Elizabeth stopped in the middle of a sob, but she was cleverer now, and she argued. "Why?" asked Elizabeth.

The "Ting" took no notice. "Look in the box."

"Why? It's empty."

"Look in the box."

"It's *empty*."

"Look."

It was more than a "Ting". It was a stir, as if the box were alive, as if – a wand were waving?

Slowly Elizabeth put out her hand. The lid of the box flew off – "Did I open it?" asked Elizabeth. She heard the blue tissue paper rustle – "Did I rustle it?" – and out, in her hand, came Fairy Doll.

"But how?" asked Christabel. "How? And how did Elizabeth *know*? I just said, 'What shall we put on top?' and –"

"She ran straight upstairs," said Godfrey, "and came back with Fairy Doll –"

"Who was lost," said Josie. "Wasn't she lost?"

"We don't understand," they said, all three together. You may think that when Josie was jealous she stole Fairy Doll and put her back in the cedar chest. Then why was Josie so surprised? And how was it that Fairy Doll was not draggled at all, but clean, in a fresh new dress, with new silver wings and another pair of mice-sewn shoes?

Perhaps it was Mother who found her and put her away because it was time that Elizabeth had "Tings" of her own. Mother could have made the dress and wings, but, "I couldn't have sewn those shoes," said Mother.

Fairy Doll looked straight in front of her, and the wand stirred gently, very gently in her hand.

Fairy Doll went back in her place on the top of the Christmas tree. After Christmas she was laid away in the cedar chest till next year. "She has done her work," said Mother.

Christabel had her writing case; Godfrey had his engine; Josie, who was cured of being jealous, had a kitchen set with pots and pans, a pastry board, a rolling pin, and a kettle. Elizabeth had a long-clothes baby doll, with eyes that opened and shut.

She loves the baby doll, but every time she goes up and down the stairs she stops on the landing and puts her hand on the cedar chest; every time she does it – it may be her imagination – from inside comes a faint glass "Ting" that is like a Christmas bell.

The Story
of Holly
and Ivy

This is a story about wishing. It is also about a doll and a little girl. It begins with the doll.

Her name, of course, was Holly.

It could not have been anything else, for she was dressed for Christmas in a red dress, and red shoes, though her petticoat and socks were green.

She was ten inches high and carefully jointed; she had real gold hair, brown glass eyes, and teeth like tiny china pearls.

It was the morning of Christmas Eve, the last day before Christmas. The toys in Mr Blossom's toy shop in the little country town stirred and shook themselves after the long night. "We must be sold today," they said.

"Today?" asked Holly. She had been unpacked only the day before and was the newest toy in the shop.

Outside in the street it was snowing but the toy-shop window was lit and warm – it had been lit all night. The tops showed their glinting colours, the balls their bands of red and yellow and blue; the trains were ready to run round and round. There were steamboats and electric boats; the sailing boats shook out their fresh white sails. The clockwork toys had each its private key; the tea sets gleamed in their boxes. There were aeroplanes, trumpets, and doll perambulators; the rocking-horses looked as if they were prancing, and the teddy bears held up their furry arms. There was every kind of stuffed animal – rabbits and lions and tigers, dogs and cats, even turtles with real shells. The dolls were on a long glass shelf decorated with tinsel – baby dolls and bride dolls, with bridesmaids in every colour, a boy doll in a kilt and another who was a sailor. One girl doll was holding her gloves, another had an umbrella. They were all beautiful, but none of them had been sold.

"We must be sold today," said the dolls.

"Today?" said Holly.

Like the teddy bears, the dolls held out their arms. Toys, of course, think the opposite way to you. "We shall have a little boy or girl for Christmas," said the toys.

"Will I?" asked Holly.

"We shall have homes."

"Will I?" asked Holly.

The toys knew what homes were like from the broken dolls who came to the shop to be mended. "There are warm fires and lights," said the dolls, "rooms filled with lovely things. We feel children's hands."

"Bah! Children's hands are rough," said the big toy owl who sat on a pretend branch below the dolls. "They are rough. They can squeeze."

"I want to be squeezed," said a little elephant.

"We have never felt a child's hands," said two baby

69

hippopotamuses. They were made of grey velvet, and their pink velvet mouths were open and as wide as the rest of them. Their names were Mallow and Wallow. "We have never felt a child's hands."

Neither, of course, had Holly.

The owl's name was Abracadabra. He was so big and important that he thought the toy shop belonged to him.

"I thought it belonged to Mr Blossom," said Holly.

"Hsst! T-whoo!" said Abracadabra, which was his way of being cross. "Does a new little doll dare to speak?"

"Be careful. Be careful," the dolls warned Holly.

Abracadabra had widespread wings marked with yellow and brown, a big hooked beak, and white felt feet like claws. Above his eyes were two fierce black tufts, and the eyes themselves were so big and green that they made green shadows on his round white cheeks. His eyes saw everything, even at night. Even the biggest toys were afraid of Abracadabra. Mallow and Wallow shook on their round stubby feet each time he spoke.

"He might think we're mice," said Mallow and Wallow.

"My mice," said Abracadabra.

"Mr Blossom's mice," said Holly.

Holly's place on the glass shelf was quite close to Abracadabra. He gave her a look with his green eyes.

"This is the last day for shopping," said Abracadabra. "Tomorrow the shop will be shut."

A shiver went round all the dolls, but Holly knew Abracadabra was talking to her.

"But the fathers and mothers will come today," said the little elephant. He was called Crumple because his skin did not fit but hung in comfortable folds round his neck and his knees. He had a scarlet flannel saddle hung with bells, and his trunk, his mouth, and his tail all turned up, which gave him a cheerful expression. It was easy for Crumple to be cheerful; on his saddle was a ticket marked "Sold". He had only to be made into a parcel.

"Will I be a parcel?" asked Holly.

"I am sure you will," said Crumple, and he waved his trunk at her and told the dolls, "You will be put into Christmas stockings."

"Oooh!" said the dolls, longingly.

"Or hung on Christmas trees."

"Aaaah!" said the dolls.

"But you won't all be sold," said Abracadabra, and Holly knew he was talking to her.

The sound of a key in the lock was heard. It was Mr Blossom come to open the shop. Peter the shop boy was close behind him. "We shall be busy today," said Mr Blossom.

"Yes sir," said Peter.

There could be no more talking, but, "We can wish.

We *must* wish," whispered the dolls, and Holly whispered, "I *am* wishing."

"Hoo! Hoo!" went Abracadabra. It did not matter if Peter and Mr Blossom heard him; it was his toy-owl sound. "Hoo! Hoo!" They did not know but the toys all knew that it was Abracadabra's way of laughing.

The toys thought that all children have homes, but all children have not.

Far away in the city was a big house called St Agnes's, where thirty boys and girls had to live together, but now, for three days, they were saying "Good-bye" to St Agnes's. "A kind lady – or gentleman – has asked for you for Christmas," Miss Shepherd, who looked after them all, had told them, and one by one the children were called for or taken to the train. Soon there would be no one left in the big house but Miss Shepherd and Ivy.

Ivy was a little girl six years old with straight hair cut in a fringe, blue-grey eyes, and a turned-up nose. She had a green coat the colour of her name, and red gloves, but no lady or gentleman had asked for her for Christmas. "I don't care," said Ivy.

Sometimes in Ivy there was an empty feeling, and the emptiness ached; it ached so much that she had to say something quickly in case she cried, and, "I don't care at all," said Ivy.

"You will care," said the last boy, Barnabas, who was

waiting for a taxi. "Cook has gone, the maids have gone, and Miss Shepherd is going to her sister. You will care," said Barnabas.

"I won't," said Ivy, and she said more quickly, "I'm going to my grandmother."

"You haven't got a grandmother," said Barnabas. "We don't have them." That was true. The boys and girls at St Agnes's had no fathers and mothers, let alone grand-mothers.

"But I have," said Ivy. "At Aylesbury."

I do not know how that name came into Ivy's head. Perhaps she had heard it somewhere. She said it again. "In Aylesbury."

"Bet you haven't," said Barnabas, and he went on saying that until his taxi came.

When Barnabas had gone Miss Shepherd said, "Ivy, I shall have to send you to the country, to our Infants' Home."

"Infants are babies," said Ivy. "I'm not a baby."

But Miss Shepherd only said, "There is nowhere else for you to go."

"I'll go to my grandmother," said Ivy.

"You haven't got a grandmother," said Miss Shepherd. "I'm sorry to send you to the Infants' Home, for there won't be much for you to see there or anyone to talk to, but I don't know what else to do with you. My sister has influenza and I have to go and nurse her."

"I'll help you," said Ivy.

"You might catch it," said Miss Shepherd. "That wouldn't do." And she took Ivy to the station and put her on the train.

She put Ivy's suitcase in the rack and gave her a packet of sandwiches, an apple, a ticket, two shillings, and a parcel that was her Christmas present; onto Ivy's coat she pinned a label with the address of the Infants' Home. "Be a good girl," said Miss Shepherd.

When Miss Shepherd had gone Ivy tore the label off and threw it out of the window. "I'm going to my grandmother," said Ivy.

All day long people came in and out of the toy shop. Mr Blossom and Peter were so busy they could hardly snatch a cup of tea.

Crumple was made into a parcel and taken away; teddy bears and sailing ships were brought out of the window; dolls were lifted down from the shelf. The boy doll in the kilt and the doll with gloves were sold, and baby dolls and brides.

Holly held out her arms and smiled her china smile. Each time a little girl came to the window and looked, pressing her face against the glass, Holly asked, "Are *you* my Christmas girl?" Each time the shop door opened she was sure it was for her.

"I am here. I am Holly;" and she wished, "Ask for me. Lift me down. *Ask!*" But nobody asked.

"Hoo! Hoo!" said Abracadabra.

Ivy was still in the train. She had eaten her sandwiches almost at once and opened her present. She had hoped and believed she would have a doll this Christmas, but the present was a pencil box. A doll would have filled up the emptiness – and now it ached so much that Ivy had to press her lips together tightly, and, "My grandmother will give me a doll," she said out loud.

"Will she, dear?" asked a lady sitting opposite, and the people in the carriage all looked at Ivy and smiled. "And where does your grandmother live?" asked a gentleman.

"In Aylesbury," said Ivy.

The lady nodded. "That will be two or three stations," she said.

Then . . . there *is* an Aylesbury, thought Ivy.

The lady got out, more people got in, and the train went on. Ivy grew sleepy watching the snowflakes fly past the window. The train seemed to be going very fast, and she leaned her head against the carriage cushions and shut her eyes. When she opened them the train had stopped at a small station and the people in her carriage were all getting out. The gentleman lifted her suitcase down from the rack. "A....b..y," said the notice boards. Ivy could not read very well but she knew A was for "Aylesbury".

Forgetting all about her suitcase and the pencil box, she jumped down from the train, slammed the carriage door behind her, and followed the crowd of people as they went through the station gate. The ticket-collector had so many tickets he did not look at hers; in a moment Ivy was out in the street, and the train had chuffed out of the station. "I don't care," said Ivy. "This is where my grandmother lives."

The country town looked pleasant and clean after the city. There were cobbled streets going up and down, and houses with gables overhanging the pavements and roofs jumbled together. Some of the houses had windows with many small panes; some had doors with brass knockers. The paint was bright and the curtains clean. "I like where my grandmother lives," said Ivy.

Presently she came to the market square where the Christmas market was going on. There were stalls of turkeys and geese, fruit stalls with oranges, apples, nuts, and tangerines that are like small oranges wrapped in silver paper. Some stalls had holly, mistletoe, and Christmas trees, some had flowers; there were stalls of china and glass and one with wooden spoons and bowls. A woman was selling balloons and an old man was cooking hot chestnuts. Men were shouting, the women had shopping bags and baskets, the children were running, everyone was buying or selling and laughing. Ivy had spent all her life in St Agnes's; she had not seen a market before; and, "I won't look for my grandmother yet," said Ivy.

In the toy shop Mr Blossom had never made so much money, Peter had never worked so hard. Peter was fif-

teen; he had red cheeks and a smile as wide as Mallow's and Wallow's; he took good care of the toys and did everything he could to help Mr Blossom. *Whish!* went the brown paper as Peter pulled it off the roll, *whirr!* went the string ball, *snip-snap*, the scissors cut off the string. He did up dozens of parcels, ran up and down the stepladder, fetched and carried and took away. "That abominable boy will sell every toy in the shop," grumbled Abracadabra.

"What's abominable?" asked Holly.

"It means not good," said the dolls, "but he is good. Dear, dear Peter!" whispered the dolls, but Abracadabra's green eyes had caught the light from a passing car. They gave a flash and, rattle-bang! Peter fell down the stepladder from top to bottom. He bumped his elbow, grazed his knee, and tore a big hole in his pocket. "Hold on! Go slow!" said Mr Blossom.

"Yes sir," said poor Peter in a very little voice.

"Did you see that, did you see *that?*" whispered the dolls. Holly wished she were farther away from Abracadabra.

Soon all the baby dolls but one were sold and most of the teddy bears. Mallow and Wallow were taken for twin boys' stockings; they were done up in two little parcels and carried away. Hardly a ball was left, and not a single aeroplane. The sailor doll was sold, and the doll with the umbrella, but still no one had asked for Holly.

Dolls are not like us; we are alive as soon as we are born, but dolls are not really alive until they are played with. "I want to be played with," said Holly, "I want someone to move my arms and legs, to make me open and shut my eyes. I wish! I wish!" said Holly.

It began to be dark. The dusk made the lighted window shine so brightly that everyone stopped to look in. The children pressed their faces so closely against the glass that the tips of their noses looked like white cherries. Holly held out her arms and smiled her china smile, but the children walked away. "Stop. Stop," wished Holly, but they did not stop.

Abracadabra's eyes shone in the dusk. Holly began to be very much afraid.

One person stopped, but it was not a boy or girl. It was Mrs Jones, the policeman's wife from down the street. She was passing the toy shop on her way home when Holly's red dress caught her eye. "Pretty!" said Mrs Jones, and stopped.

You and I would have felt Holly's wish at once, but Mrs Jones had no children and it was so long since she had known a doll that she did not understand; only a feeling stirred in her that she had not had for a long time, a feeling of Christmas, and when she got home she told Mr Jones, "This year we shall have a tree."

"Don't be daft," said Mr Jones, but when Mrs Jones had put her shopping away, a chicken and a small plum-pudding for her and Mr Jones's Christmas dinner, a piece of fish for the cat, and a dozen fine handkerchiefs which were Mr Jones's present, she went back to the market and bought some holly, mistletoe, and a Christmas tree.

"A tree should have tinsel," said Mrs Jones. She bought some tinsel. "And candles," she said. "Candles are prettier than electric light." She bought twelve red candles. "They need candle clips," she said, and bought twelve of those. And a tree should have some balls, thought Mrs Jones, glass balls in jewel colours, ruby-red, emerald-green, and gold. She bought some balls and a box of tiny silver crackers and a tinsel star. When she got home she stood the tree in the window and dressed it, putting the star on the top.

"Who is to look at it?" asked Mr Jones.

Mrs Jones thought for a moment and said, "Christmas needs children, Albert." Albert was Mr Jones's name. "I wonder," said Mrs Jones. "Couldn't we find a little girl?"

"What's the matter with you today, my dear?" said Mr Jones. "How could we find a little girl? You're daft." And it was a little sadly that Mrs Jones put holly along the chimney shelf, hung mistletoe in the hall, tied a bunch of holly on the door knocker, and went back to her housework.

Ivy was happy in the market. She walked round and

round the stalls, looking at all the things; sometimes a snowflake fell on her head, but she shook it off; sometimes one stuck to her cheek, but she put out her tongue and licked it away. She bought a bag of chestnuts from the chestnut man; they were hot in her hands and she ate them one by one. She had a cup of tea from a tea stall on wheels, and from a sweet stall she bought a toffee apple. When her legs grew tired she sat down on a step and wrapped the ends of her coat round her knees. When she was cold she started to walk again.

Soon lights were lit all along the stalls; they looked like stars. The crowd grew thicker. People laughed and stamped in the snow to keep their feet warm; Ivy stamped too. The stall-keepers shouted and called for people to come and buy. Ivy bought a blue balloon.

At St Agnes's a telegraph boy rang the bell. He had a telegram for Miss Shepherd from the Infants' Home. It said, IVY NOT ARRIVED. SUPPOSE SHE IS WITH YOU. MERRY CHRISTMAS.

The boy rang and rang, but there was no one at St Agnes's to answer the bell, and at last he put a notice in the letter box, got on his bicycle, and rode away.

In her house down the street Mrs Jones kept looking at the Christmas tree. "Oughtn't there to be presents?" she asked. It was so long since she had had a tree of her own that she could not be sure. She took Mr Jones's handkerchiefs, wrapped them in white paper and tied them with some red ribbon she had by her, and put the parcel at the foot of the tree. That looked better but still not quite right.

"There ought to be toys," said Mrs Jones, and she called to Mr Jones, "Albert!"

Mr Jones looked up from the newspaper he was reading.

"Would it be very silly, Albert?" asked Mrs Jones.

"Would *what* be silly?"

"Would it be silly to buy . . . a little doll?"

"What *is* the matter with you today?" asked Mr Jones, and he said again, "You're daft."

Soon it was time for him to go on duty.

"I shall be out all night," he told Mrs Jones. "Two of the men are away sick. I shall take a short sleep at the police station and go on duty again. See you in the morning," said Mr Jones.

He kissed Mrs Jones good-bye and went out, but put his head round the door again. "Have a good breakfast waiting for me," said Mr Jones.

In the toy shop it was closing time.

"What does that mean?" asked Holly.

"That it's over," said Abracadabra.

"Over?" Holly did not understand.

Mr Blossom pulled the blind down on the door and put up a notice: "Closed".

"Closed. Hoo! Hoo!" said Abracadabra.

Mr Blossom was so tired he told Peter to tidy the shop. "And you can lock up. Can I trust you?" asked Mr Blossom.

"Yes sir," said Peter.

"Be careful of the key," said Mr Blossom.

"Yes sir," said Peter proudly. It was the first time Mr Blossom had trusted him with the key.

"You have been a good boy," said Mr Blossom as he was going. "You may choose any toy you like – except the expensive ones like air guns or electric trains. Yes, choose yourself a toy," said Mr Blossom. "Good night."

When Mr Blossom had gone; "A toy!" said Peter, and he asked, "What does he think I am? A blooming kid?"

Peter swept up the bits of paper and string and straw and put them in the rubbish bin at the back of the shop. He was so tired he forgot to put the lid on the bin. Then he dusted the counter, but he was too tired to do any more, so he put on his overcoat to go home. He turned out the lights – it was no use lighting the window now that the shopping was over – stepped outside, and closed and locked the door. If he had waited a moment he would have heard a stirring, a noise, tiny whimperings. "What about us? What about us?" It was the toys.

"Go home and good riddance!" said Abracadabra to Peter; but the toys cried, "Don't go! Don't go!"

Peter heard nothing. He put the key in his jacket pocket to keep it quite safe and turned to run home.

The key fell straight through the torn pocket into the snow. It did not make a sound.

"Hoo! Hoo!" said Abracadabra, and the snowflakes began to cover the key as Peter ran off.

The market was over as well. The crowd had gone, the stalls were packing up, the last Christmas trees were being sold. Ivy had spent all her money, the blue balloon had burst, her legs ached with tiredness, and she shivered.

Then the lights went out; there were only pools of yellow from the lamp posts, with patches of darkness between. A bit of paper blew against Ivy's legs, making her jump. Suddenly the market place seemed large and strange; she would have liked to see Miss Shepherd.

Many little girls would have cried but Ivy was not that kind of little girl. Though the empty feeling ached inside her she pressed her lips tightly together, then said, "It's time I looked for my grandmother," and started off to look.

She walked up the cobbled streets between the houses.

How cozy they seemed, with their lighted windows; smoke was going up from every chimney. "There are fires and beds and supper," said Ivy. Some of the houses had wreaths of holly on their front doors, paper chains and garlands in their rooms; and in almost every window was a Christmas tree.

When Ivy looked in she could see children. In one house they were sitting round a table, eating; in another they were hanging stockings from the chimney shelf; in some they were doing up parcels, but, "I must look for a house with a tree and no children," said Ivy.

She knew there would be a tree, "Because my grandmother is expecting me," said Ivy.

The toy shop was still and dark. "Thank goodness!" said Abracadabra.

"But people can't see us," said Holly.

"Why should they see us?" asked Abracadabra. "It's over. People have all gone home. The children are going to bed." He sounded pleased. "There will be no more shopping," said Abracadabra, and the whisper ran round the toys, "No shopping. No shopping."

"Then . . . we are the ones not sold," said a doll.

There was a long silence.

"I can be sold any time," said a bride doll at last. "Weddings are always."

"I am in yellow, with primroses," said a bridesmaid. "I shall be sold in the spring."

"I am in pink, with roses," said another. "They will buy me in the summer." But Holly had a red dress, for Christmas. What would be done with her?

"You will be put back into stock," said Abracadabra.

"Please . . . what is stock?" whispered Holly.

"It is shut up and dark," said Abracadabra, as if he liked that very much. "No one sees you or disturbs you. You get covered with dust, and I shall be there," said Abracadabra.

Holly wished she could crack.

"*This* is my grandmother's house," said Ivy, but when she got to the house it was not. That happened several times. "Then it's that one," she said, but it was not that one either. She began to be very cold and tired.

Somebody came down the street. Even in the snow his tread was loud. It was a big policeman. (As a matter of fact, it was Mr Jones.)

Ivy knew as well as you or I know that policemen are kind people and do not like little girls to wander about alone after dark in a strange town. "He might send me to the Infants' Home," said Ivy and, quick as a mouse going into its hole, she whisked into a passage between two shops.

"Queer!" said Mr Jones. "I thought I saw something green."

At the end of the passage was a shed, and Ivy whisked into it and stood behind the door. There was something odd about that shed – it was warm. Ivy did not know how an empty shed could be warm on a cold night, but I shall tell you.

The shed belonged to a baker and was built against the

wall behind his oven. All day he had been baking bread and rolls for Christmas, and the oven was still hot. When Ivy put her hand on the wall she had to take it away quickly, for the wall was baking-hot.

Soon she stopped shivering. In a corner was a pile of flour sacks, and she sat down on them.

A lamp in the passageway outside gave just enough light. Ivy's legs began to feel heavy and warm; her fingers and toes seemed to uncurl and stretch in the warmth, while her eyelids seemed to curl up. She gave a great yawn.

Then she took off her coat, lay down on the sacks, and spread the coat over her.

In a moment she was fast asleep.

The toy shop was close by the passage. It was too dark to be noticed, though Abracadabra's eyes shone like green lamps.

"Shopping is over. Hoo! Hoo!" said Abracadabra.

"Over. Over," mourned the toys.

They did not know and Abracadabra did not know that it is when shopping is over that Christmas begins.

Soon it was not dark, for the snow had stopped and the moon came up and lighted all the town. The roofs sparkled with frost as did the snow on the pavements and roads. In the toy-shop window the toys showed, not as bright as day, but bright as moonlight, which is far more beautiful. Holly's dress looked a pale red, and her hair was pale gold.

Dolls do not lie down to go to sleep; they only do that when you remember to put them to bed and, as you often forget, they would be tired if they had to wait; they can sleep where they stand or sit, and now the dolls in the toy-shop window slept in their places, all but Holly. She could not go to sleep. She was a Christmas doll and it was beginning to be Christmas. She could not know why, but she was excited. Then all at once, softly, bells began to ring.

Long after most children are in bed, on Christmas Eve, the church bells in towns and villages begin to ring. Soon the clocks strike twelve and it is Christmas.

Holly heard the bells and – what was this? People were walking in the street – hurrying. "Hsst! T-whoo!" said Abracadabra at them as they passed, but they took no notice.

"Then . . . it has started," said Holly.

"What has started?" said Abracadabra.

"It," said Holly. She could not explain better than that for she did not know yet what "it" meant – this was, after all, her first Christmas – but the bells grew louder and more and more people passed. Then, it may have been the pin of Holly's price ticket, or a spine of tinsel come loose from the shelf, but Holly felt a tiny pricking as sharp as a prickle on a holly leaf. "Wish," said the prickle. "Wish."

"But – the shop is closed," said Holly. "The children

are in bed. Abracadabra says I must go into sto—" The prickle interrupted. "Wish. Wish!" said the prickle. "Wish!" It went on till Holly wished.

Ivy thought the bells woke her or perhaps the passing feet, but then why did she feel something sharp like a thistle or a hard straw in one of the sacks? She sat up, but she was half asleep and she thought the feet were the St Agnes's children marching down to breakfast and the bells were the breakfast bell. Then she saw she was still in the shed, though it was filled with a new light, a strange silver light. "Moonlight?" asked Ivy and rubbed her eyes. She was warm and comfortable on the sacks under the green coat – though there were great white patches on it from the flour – too warm and comfortable to move, and she lay down, but again she felt that thistle or sharp straw. The light seemed to be calling her, the bells, the hurrying feet; the prickle seemed to tell her to get up.

Ivy put on her coat and went out.

Outside in the passage the footsteps sounded so loud that she guessed it was the policeman. She waited until they had passed before she dared come out.

In the street the moonlight was so bright that once again Ivy thought it was morning and she was in St Agnes's and the bells were the breakfast bell. "Only . . . there are so many of them," said sleepy Ivy.

She walked a few steps to the toy shop. She did not

know how it came to be there and she thought she was in her St Agnes's bedroom and it was filled with toys. Then: "Not *toys*," said Ivy, "*a* toy," and she was wide awake. She did not even see Abracadabra glaring at her with his green eyes; she looked straight at Holly.

She saw Holly's dress and socks and shoes. She is red and green too, thought Ivy. She saw Holly's hair, brown eyes, little teeth, and beautiful joints. They were just what Ivy liked, and, "My Christmas doll!" said Ivy.

Holly saw Ivy's face pressed against the window as she had seen so many children's faces that day, but, "This one is different," said Holly.

Ivy's hands in their woollen gloves held to the ledge where it said BLOSSOM, HIGH-CLASS TOYS AND GAMES. Holly looked at Ivy's hands. Soon they will be holding me, thought Holly. Ivy's coat even in the moonlight was as beautiful a green as Holly's dress was a beautiful red, so that they seemed to match, and, "My Christmas girl!" said Holly.

Ivy had to go to the shed again to get warm, but I cannot tell you how many times she came back to look at Holly.

"My Christmas doll!"

"My Christmas girl!"

"But the window is between," said Abracadabra.

The window was in between and the toy-shop door was locked, but even if it had been open Ivy had no money. "Hoo! Hoo!" said Abracadabra, but, remember, not only Holly but Ivy was wishing now.

"I wish . . ."

"I wish . . ."

The toys woke up. "A child," they whispered, "a child." And they wished too.

Wishes are powerful things. Ivy stepped back from the window and Abracadabra's eyes grew pale as, cr-*runch* went something under Ivy's heel. It was something hidden just under the snow.

"Hsst!" said Abracadabra. "T-whoo!" But Ivy bent down and picked up a key.

In the moonlight it was bright silver. "Peter's key. Peter's key," whispered the toys.

Footsteps sounded in the street, people were coming from church; Ivy put the key in her pocket and quickly ran back to the shed.

She had to wait a long time for the people to pass as they stopped to say "Merry Christmas" to one another, to give each other parcels; and Ivy sat down on the sacks to rest. Presently she gave another great yawn. Presently she lay down and spread her coat over her. Presently she went to sleep.

The toys had gone to sleep too. "But I can't," said Holly. "I must wait for my Christmas girl."

She stayed awake for a long time, but she was only a little doll . . . and presently she fell asleep where she stood.

Ivy dreamed that the shed was hung with holly wreaths and lit with candles. The berries were the colour of the Christmas doll's dress and the candle flames were as bright as her hair. "A-aaah!" said Ivy.

Holly dreamed that two arms were cradling her, that hands were holding her, that her dress was beginning to be rumpled and her eyes made to open and shut. "A-aaah!" said Holly.

Abracadabra kept his green eyes wide open, but he could not stop the moon from going down, nor the coming of Christmas Day.

Very early on Christmas morning Mrs Jones got up and tidied her living room. She lit a fire, swept the hearth, and dusted the furniture. She laid a table for breakfast with a pink and white cloth, her best blue china, a loaf of crusty bread, a pat of new butter in a glass dish, honey in a blue pot, a bowl of sugar, and a jug of milk. She had some fresh brown eggs and, in the kitchen, she put sausages to sizzle in a pan. Then she set the teapot to warm on the hob, lighted the candles on the Christmas tree, and sat down by the fire to wait.

The baker's oven cooled in the night and Ivy woke with the cold. The shed was icy; Ivy's eye-lashes were stuck together with rime, and the tip of her nose felt frozen. When she tried to stand up, her legs were so stiff that she almost fell over; when she put on her coat her fingers were so numb that they could not do up the buttons. Ivy was

a sensible little girl; she knew she had to get warm and she did not cry, but, "I m-must h-hop and sk-skip," she said through her chattering teeth, and there in the shed she swung her arms, in-out, out-in, and clapped her hands. Outside she tried to run, but her legs felt heavy and her head seemed to swim. "I m-must f-find m-my g-grandmother qu-qu-quickly," said Ivy.

She went into the street, and how cold it was there! The wind blew under her coat; the snow on the pavements had turned to ice and was slippery. She tried to hop, but the snow was like glass. Ivy's fingers and nose hurt in the cold. "If-f I l-look at m-my d-d-doll, I m-might-t f-feel b-b-b-better," said Ivy, but she turned the wrong way.

It was the wrong way for the toy shop, but perhaps it was the right way for Ivy, for a hundred yards down the street she came to the Joneses' house.

I must look for a house with a tree and no children. That is what she had said. Now she looked in at the window and there was no sign of any children but there was a Christmas tree lit. Ivy saw the fire – "To w-warm m-me," whispered Ivy, and, oh, she was cold! She saw the table with the pink and white cloth, blue china, bread and butter, honey and milk, the teapot warming – "My b-breakfast," whispered Ivy and, oh, she was hungry! She saw Mrs Jones sitting by the fire, in her clean apron, waiting. Ivy stood quite still. Then: "My g-g-grandmother," whispered Ivy.

Holly woke with a start. "Oh! I have been asleep," said Holly in dismay. "Oh! I must have missed my little Christmas girl."

"*She* won't come back," said Abracadabra. "It's Christmas Day. She's playing with her new toys."

"I am her new toy," said Holly.

"Hoo! Hoo!" said Abracadabra.

"I am," said Holly, and she wished. I think her wish was bigger than Abracadabra's, for when Ivy lifted her hand to Mrs Jones's knocker, a prickle from the bunch of holly ran into her finger. "Ow!" said Ivy. The prickle was so sharp that she took her hand down, and, "F-first I must g-get my d-d-doll," said Ivy.

If Ivy had stopped to think she would have known she could not get her doll. How could she when the shop was locked and the window was in between? Besides, Holly was not Ivy's doll and had not even been sold. A wise person would have known this, but sometimes it is better to feel a prickle than to be wise.

"Hullo," said Ivy to Holly through the toy-shop window. "G-g-good morning."

Holly could not say "Hullo" back, but she could wish Ivy good morning – with a doll's wish.

In the daylight Holly was even more beautiful than she had been by moonlight, Ivy was even dearer.

"A little girl!" sneered Abracadabra. "There are hundreds of little girls."

"Not for me," said Holly.

"A little doll!" sneered Abracadabra. "There are hundreds of little dolls," and if Ivy could have heard him through the window she would have said, "Not for me."

Ivy gazed at Holly through the window.

She gazed so hard she did not hear footsteps coming down the street, heavy steps and light ones and a queer snuffling sound. The heavy steps were Mr Jones's, the light ones were Peter's, and the snuffling sound was Peter trying not to cry.

"I put it in my pocket," Peter was saying. "I forgot my pocket was torn. Oh, what shall I do? What shall I do?" said Peter.

Mr Jones patted his shoulder and asked, "What sort of key was it now?"

A key? Ivy turned round. She saw Mr Jones and jumped. Then she made herself as small as she could against the window.

"A big iron key, but it looked like silver," said Peter. He and Mr Jones began to look along the pavement.

It looked like silver. Ivy could feel the edges of the key in her pocket, but – If I go away softly the policeman won't notice me, thought Ivy.

"Mr Blossom trusted me," said Peter. His wide smile was gone and his face looked quite pale. I don't like boys, thought Ivy, but Peter was saying, "He trusted me. He'll never trust me again," and though Peter was a big boy, when he said that he looked as if he really might burst into tears.

"A boy cry?" asked Ivy. She had never seen Barnabas cry. I didn't know boys could, thought Ivy.

The toys had all wakened up again. "Poor Peter. Poor Peter"; and the whisper ran round:

"Wish. Wish Peter may find the key. Wish."

"For that careless boy?" said Abracadabra. "Why, he might have had us all stolen."

Peter was saying that himself "A thief might have picked it up," he said.

"It w-wasn't a th-thief. It was m-m-me," said Ivy and put her hand in her pocket and pulled out the key. "S-so you n-needn't c-c-cry," said Ivy to Peter.

Can you imagine how Peter's tears disappeared and his smile came back? "Cry? Cry? Who'd cry?" said Peter scornfully, and Ivy thought it better not to say, "You."

Mr Jones put the key in the lock, and it fitted. "I suppose I had better go in," said Peter, "and see if everything's all right."

"Well, I'm going home," said Mr Jones. "You know where I live. If anything's wrong, pop in." It was as he turned to go home that Mr Jones saw Ivy. "So – there *was* something green," said Mr Jones.

Ivy knew how she must look; her coat and her hair, her socks and her shoes were dusted with flour from the sacks, she had not been able to comb her hair because she had no comb, her face had smears across it from the toffee apple; and, "I think you are lost," said Mr Jones.

His voice was so kind that the empty feeling ached in Ivy; it felt so empty that her mouth began to tremble. She could not shut her lips, but, "I'm n-not l-lost," said Ivy. "I'm g-g-going to m-my g-g-g-grandmother."

"I see," said Mr Jones. He looked at Ivy again. "Where does your grandmother live?" asked Mr Jones.

"H-here," said Ivy.

"Show me," said Mr Jones and held out his hand.

Ivy took his hand and led him down the street to the Joneses' house. "This is m-my g-g-grandmother's," said Ivy.

Mr Jones seemed rather surprised. "Are you sure?" asked Mr Jones.

"Qu-quite sure," said Ivy. "She has m-my b-breakfast ready."

"Did you say . . . your breakfast?" asked Mr Jones.

"Of course," said Ivy, "L-look in at the w-window. There," she told him. "Th-there's my Ch-Christmas t-tree."

Mr Jones thought a moment. Then: "Perhaps it is your Christmas tree," he said.

"Sh-shall we kn-knock?" asked Ivy, but, "You needn't knock," said Mr Jones. "You can come in."

The toys were all in their places when Peter opened the door. "No thanks to you," said Abracadabra.

Perhaps Peter heard him, for Peter said, "Thanks to

that little girl."

I do not know how it was, but Peter had the idea that Ivy was Mr Jones's little girl. "He was kind to me," said Peter, "and so was she." Peter was very grateful, and, "What can I do for them?" he asked. Then: "I know," said Peter. Mr Blossom had told him to take any toy, and "I'll take her a doll," said Peter. "I can slip it into their house easy, without saying a word, but – what doll would she like?" asked Peter.

The toys all held their breath. "What doll would she like?"

"A bride doll," said Abracadabra with a gleam of his eyes.

A bride doll was standing on the counter, and Peter went to pick her up, but he must have put his hand on the pin of her price ticket or a wire in the orange-blossom flowers on her dress, for, "Ow!" said Peter and drew back his hand.

Abracadabra looked at Holly. Holly smiled.

"All little girls like baby dolls," said Abracadabra. "Take her a baby doll."

There was one baby doll left. She was in the window; Peter reached to take her out, but the safety-pin on the baby doll's bib must have been undone, for, "*Ow!*" cried Peter and drew back his hand.

"Hsst! T-whoo!" said Abracadabra to Holly. Holly smiled.

It was the same with the primrose bridesmaid. "Ow!"

cried Peter. The same with the rose. "Ow!" And, "Here, I'm getting fed up," said Peter. "Who's trying this on?" I do not know what made him look at Abracadabra. Abracadabra's eyes gleamed, but in her place just above Abracadabra, Peter saw Holly.

"Why, of course! The little red Christmas doll," said Peter. "The very thing!" But as he stepped up to the glass shelf Abracadabra was there.

Peter said that Abracadabra must have toppled, for a toy owl cannot fly, but it seemed for a moment that Abracadabra was right in his face; the green eyes were close, the spread wings, the hooked beak, and the claws. Peter let out a cry and hit Abracadabra, who fell on the floor. "Out of my way!" cried Peter, and he gave Abracadabra a kick. Then Abracadabra did fly. He went sailing across the shop and landed head down in the rubbish bin.

"Oooh! Aaah!" cried all the toys in terror, but Peter sprang after him and shut the lid down tight.

Then he picked up Holly from the shelf in the window and ran pellmell to the Joneses'.

When Mr Jones and Ivy came in Mrs Jones was in the kitchen with a fork in her hand, turning the sausages. Mr Jones told Ivy to wait in the hall.

"Merry Christmas," said Mr Jones to Mrs Jones and kissed her.

"Merry Christmas," said Mrs Jones, but she sounded

a little sad.

Mr Jones had a present in his pocket for Mrs Jones, a little gold brooch. He took it out, unwrapped it, and pinned it to her dress. "Oh, how pretty, Albert!" said Mrs Jones, but she still sounded sad.

"I have *another* Christmas present for you," said Mr Jones and laughed. "It has two legs," said Mr Jones.

"Two *legs?*" asked Mrs Jones, and Mr Jones laughed again.

"It can walk and talk," said Mr Jones and laughed still more, and then he brought Ivy in.

When Mrs Jones saw Ivy she did not laugh; for a moment she stood still, then she dropped the fork and knelt down on the floor and put her hands on Ivy's shoulders. "Oh, Albert!" said Mrs Jones. "Albert!" She looked at Ivy for a long time and tears came into her eyes and rolled down her cheeks. Ivy, with her glove, wiped the tears away and the emptiness went out of Ivy and never came back.

"Dearie me!" said Mrs Jones, getting to her feet, "what am I thinking of? You must have a hot bath at once."

"Breakfast first," said Mr Jones, and Ivy asked, "Couldn't I see my Christmas tree?"

Mrs Jones's living room was as bright and clean as it had looked through the window. The fire was warm on Ivy's legs, the table was close to her now, and in the window was the tree – "With a star on the top," whispered Ivy.

"But why, oh why," Mrs Jones was saying to Mr Jones outside the door, "why didn't I buy that little doll?"

"And the shops are shut," whispered Mr Jones. "We shall have to explain."

Ivy did not hear them. "Red candles!" she was whispering. "Silver crackers! Glass balls . . . !"

She stopped. Mrs Jones came in and gave a cry. "Well, I'll be danged!" said Mr Jones, for, at the foot of the tree, by the parcel of handkerchiefs, stood Holly.

Though Mrs Jones was a little young to be a grandmother, she and Mr Jones adopted Ivy, which means they took her as their own and, of course, Holly as well. Miss Shepherd came to visit them and arrange this. "Please tell Barnabas," said Ivy.

Mrs Jones made Ivy a green dress like Holly's red one but with a red petticoat and red socks. She made Holly a red coat like Ivy's green one and knitted her a pair of tiny green woollen gloves so that they matched when they went out.

They pass the toy shop often, but there is no Abracadabra.

"Where is the owl?" Mr Blossom had asked when the shop opened again, and Peter had to say, "I put him in the rubbish bin."

"Good gracious me!" said Mr Blossom, "get him out at once," but when they lifted the lid Abracadabra was not there.

"Sir, the dustman must have taken him away," said Peter, standing up stiff and straight. I do not know if that was true, but Abracadabra was never seen again.

"Never seen again," said the toys. They sounded happy. "Never seen again," and long, long afterwards in the toy shop they told tales of Abracadabra.

Sometimes Holly and Ivy meet Crumple, who waves his trunk at them. Once they saw Mallow and Wallow put out on a windowsill. They often see Peter and Mr Blossom; in spite of Abracadabra's disappearance, Mr Blossom trusts Peter.

"But if you had not found the key," says Peter to Ivy.

"If I had not come to look at Holly," says Ivy.

"If I had not gone to Mr Jones," says Peter.

"If Mrs Jones had not bought the Christmas tree" – but it goes farther back than that. If Ivy had not slept in the shed . . . If the baker had not lit his oven . . . If Ivy had not got out of the train . . . If Barnabas had not laughed at Ivy . . . If Holly . . .

"If I had not wished," says Holly.

I told you it was a story about wishing.

Candy
Floss

This is the tune Jack's music box played

Ah, my dear old Au-gus-tine, Au-gus-tine, Au-gus-tine,

Ah, my dear old Au-gus-tine, ev-ery-thing's gone —

Mon-ey's gone, sweet-heart's gone — all is gone, Au-gus-tine,

Ah, my dear old Au-gus-tine, ev-ery-thing's gone.

Once upon a time there was a doll who lived in a coconut shy.

You and I can say we live in London, or Chichester, or in Connecticut, France, Japan, Honolulu, or the country or town where we do live. She lived in a coconut shy.

A coconut shy is part of a fair. People come to it and pay their money to throw wooden balls at coconuts set up on posts. If anyone hits a coconut off the post he can keep it. It is quite difficult, but lots of nuts are won, and it is great fun.

This particular shy was kept by a young man called Jack.

There are many coconut shies in a fair, but Jack's was different. It had the same three-sided tent, the same red and white posts for the nuts, the same scarlet box stands for the balls; it had the same flags and notices and Jack called out the same call: "Three balls f'r threepence! Seven f'r a tanner!" (A tanner is what Jack called a sixpence.) All these were the same, but still this shy was different, for beside it, on a stool, Jack's dog sat up and begged by a little mechanical organ that Jack had found and mended till it played (he called it his music box). On top of the box was a little wooden horse, and as the music played – though it could play only one tune – the horse turned round and round and frisked up and down. On the horse's back sat a beautiful little doll.

The dog's name was Cocoa, the horse's name was Nuts, and the doll was Candy Floss.

A fair is noisy with music and shouting, with whistles and bangs and laughing and squeals as people go on the big wheel, the merry-go-rounds, or the bumper cars. Jack's music box had to play very loudly to be heard at all, but Cocoa, Nuts, and Candy Floss did not mind its noise; indeed, they liked it; no other shy had a music box, let alone a dog that begged, a horse that frisked, or a doll that turned round and round. A great many people came to Jack's shy to look at them – and stayed to buy balls and shy them at the nuts.

"We help Jack," said Candy Floss, Cocoa, and Nuts.

Jack was thin and dark and young. He wore jeans, an old coat full of holes, and an old felt hat; in his ears were golden rings.

Cocoa was brown and tufty like a poodle; he wore a collar for every day and a red, blue, and white bow for work. Cocoa's work was to guard the music box, Nuts, Candy Floss, and the old drawer where Jack kept the lolly (which was what he called money). Cocoa had also to sit on a stool and beg, but he could get down when he liked, and under the stool was a bowl marked "Dog" and filled with clean water, so that he was quite comfortable.

Nuts was painted white with black spots; his neck was

arched and he held his forelegs up. He had a black-painted mane and wore a red harness hung with bells.

Cocoa and Nuts were pretty, but prettiest of all was Candy Floss; she was made of china, with china cheeks and ears and nose, and she had a little china smile. Her eyes were glass, blue as bluebells; her hair was fine and gold, like spun toffee. She was dressed in a pink gauze skirt with a strip of gauze for a bodice. When she needed a new dress Jack would soak the old one off with hot water, fluff up a new one and stick it on with glue. On her feet were painted dancing shoes as red as bright red cherries.

The music box played:

Cocoa begged, Nuts frisked, Candy Floss turned round and round. All the children made their fathers and mothers stop to look. When they stopped, the fathers would buy balls and if anybody made a nut fall down Jack handed out a beautiful new coconut. He was kept very busy, calling out his call, picking up the balls; and the heap of pennies and sixpences in the lolly drawer grew bigger.

went the music box; Cocoa begged, Nuts frisked, and Candy Floss turned round and round.

When the coconuts were all gone Jack would empty the lolly drawer, put out the lights, and close the shy. He shut off the music box and let Cocoa get down. Nuts was covered over with an old red cloth so that he could sleep; Jack put Candy Floss into his pocket (there was a hole handy so that she could see out) and, with Cocoa at his heels, went round the fair.

They went on the big merry-go-rounds where the big steam organs played "Yankee Doodle" and "Colonel Bogey" and other tunes. Jack sat on a horse or a wooden swan, a camel or an elephant, with Cocoa on the saddle in front of him and Candy Floss safe in his pocket; round they went, helter-skelter, until Candy Floss was dizzy. The little merry-go-rounds had buses, engines, and motorcars that were too small for Jack, but sometimes Candy Floss and Cocoa sat in a car by themselves. Here the music was nursery rhymes, and the children tooted the horns. Toot. Toot-toot-toot. Candy Floss wished she could toot a horn.

Sometimes they went to the Bingo booths and tried to win prizes. Once Jack had won a silk handkerchief, bright purple printed with shamrocks in emerald-green. Cocoa and Candy Floss thought it a most beautiful prize and Jack always wore it round his neck.

Sometimes they went on the bumper cars. When the cars bumped into one another the girls shut their eyes and squealed; Candy Floss's eyes would not shut, but she would have liked to squeal.

Best of all they went on the big wheel, with its seats that went up and up in the air high over the fair and the lights, so high that Candy Floss trembled, even though she was in Jack's pocket.

When they were hungry they would eat fair food. Sometimes they ate hot dogs from the hot-dog stall; Cocoa had one to himself but Candy Floss had the tip end of Jack's. Sometimes they had fish and chips at the fried-fish bar; Cocoa had a whole fish and Candy Floss had a chip. Often they had toffee apples; Cocoa used to get his stuck on his jaw and had to stand on his head to get it off. Sometimes they had ice cream and Jack made a tiny cone out of a cigarette paper for Candy Floss.

When they were tired they came back to an old van that Jack had bought dirt cheap (which was what he called buying for very little money). He had mended it and now it would go anywhere. Jack put the music box and Nuts in the van too, so that they would all be together. Then he closed the doors and they all lay down to sleep.

Jack slept on the floor of the van on some sacks and an old sleeping bag. Cocoa slept at Jack's feet. Candy Floss slept in the empty lolly drawer which Jack put beside his

pillow; the sixpences and pennies had been put in a stocking that Jack kept in a secret place. He folded up the shamrock handkerchief to make the drawer soft for Candy Floss and tucked one end round her for a blanket.

As she lay in the drawer Candy Floss could feel Jack big and warm beside her; she could hear Cocoa breathing, and knew Nuts was under the cloth. Outside, the music of the fair went on; through the van window the stars looked like sixpences. Soon Candy Floss was fast asleep.

Fairs do not stay in one place very long, only a day, two days, perhaps a week. Then Jack would pack up the coconut shy, the lights and the flags, the posts, the nuts, the stands, and the wooden balls. He would take down the three-sided tent, put everything on the van, start it up, and drive away. The music box with Nuts travelled on the floor in front, Cocoa sat on the seat, but Candy Floss had the best place of all: Jack made the shamrock handkerchief into a sling for her and hung it on the driving mirror. Candy Floss could watch the road and see everywhere they went.

Sometimes the new fair was at a seaside town. Jack would stop the van and they would have a picnic on the beach. Cocoa would chase crabs, Nuts had some seaweed hay, and Jack found Candy Floss a shell for a plate.

Sometimes the fair was in the country and they picnicked in a wood. Cocoa chased rabbits, not crabs, Nuts had moss for straw, and Jack found Candy Floss an acorn cup for a drinking bowl.

Sometimes they stopped in a field. Cocoa would have liked to chase sheep but he did not dare. Jack made daisy-chain reins for Nuts, Candy Floss had a wild rose for a hat; but no matter where they stopped to picnic, sooner or later the van would drive on to another fairground and Jack would put up the shy.

Cocoa would be brushed and his bow put on, and he would get up on his stool while Jack filled the bowl marked "Dog". The cloth came off the music box and Nuts would be polished with a rag until he shone. Then Jack would fluff up Candy Floss's dress and with his own comb spread out her hair. He washed her face (sometimes, I am sorry to say, with spit) and sat her carefully on the saddle and switched on the music and lights. "Three f'r threepence! Seven f'r a tanner!" Jack would cry.

went the music box; Cocoa begged, Nuts frisked, and Candy Floss turned round and round.

Sometimes the other fair people laughed at Jack about what they called his toys; but, "Shut up out of that," he would say. "Toys? They're partners." (Only he said "pardners".)

"A doll for a partner? Garn!" they would jeer.

"Doll! She's my luck," said Jack.

That was true. Jack's shy had more people and took in more pennies and sixpences than any other shy.

Cocoa, Nuts, and Candy Floss were proud to be Jack's partners; Candy Floss was very proud to be his luck.

Then one Easter they came to the heath high up above London which was the biggest fair of all (a heath is a big open space, covered with grass). Only the very best shies and merry-go-rounds, the biggest wheels were there. The Bingos had expensive prizes, there was a mouse circus, three rifle ranges, and stalls where you could smash china. There were toy-sellers and balloon-sellers, paper flowers and paper umbrellas. There were rows and rows of hot-dog stalls, fish bars, and toffee-apple shops.

Cocoa had a new bow. Nuts had new silver bells. Candy Floss had a new pink dress like a cloud. Jack painted the posts and bought a pile of new coconuts.

"Goin' to make more lolly'n ever we done," said Jack. "More sixpences'n stars in the sky."

went the music box; and how well Cocoa begged, how gaily Nuts frisked, and Candy Floss turned round and round as gracefully as a dancer. More and more people began to come – hundreds of people, thought Candy

Floss. The wooden balls flew; pennies and sixpences poured into the lolly drawer.

"That's my luck!" cried Jack, and Candy Floss felt very proud.

Now not far from the heath, in a big house on the hill leading down from the heath to the town, there lived a girl called Clementina Davenport.

She was seven years old, with brown hair cut in a fringe, brown eyes, a small straight nose, and a small red mouth. She would have been pretty if she had not looked so cross. She looked cross because she *was* cross. She said she had nothing to do.

"I don't know *what* to do with Clementina," said her mother. "What can I give her to make her happy?"

Clementina had a day nursery and a night nursery all to herself, and a garden to play in. She had a nurse who was not allowed to tell her to sit up or pay attention or eat her pudding or any of the other things you and I are told.

She had a dolls' house, a white piano, cupboards full of toys, and two bookcases filled with books. She had a toy kitten in a basket, a toy poodle in another, and a real kitten and a real poodle as well. She had a cage of budgerigars and a pony to ride. Last Christmas her father gave her a pale blue bicycle, and her mother a watch, a painting box, and a painting book. Still Clementina had nothing to do.

"What *am* I to do with Clementina?" asked her mother, and she gave her a new television set and a pair of roller skates.

You might think Clementina had everything she wanted, but no, she was still quite good at wants and, on Easter Monday afternoon when the garden was full of daffodils and blossom, the sound of the fair came from the heath, over the wall, into the garden; and, "I want to go to the fair," said Clementina.

Another way in which Clementina was not like you or me was that for her "I want" was the same as "I shall".

"*Not* a nasty common fair!" said her mother.

"I *want* to go," said Clementina and stamped her foot, and so her father put on his hat, fetched his walking stick, and took her to the fair.

Of course she went on everything: on the little merry-go-rounds where she rode on a bus and wanted to change to an engine, then changed to a car and back to the bus; on the big merry-go-rounds where she rode on a swan and changed to a camel and changed to a horse. She went on the bumper cars where she did not squeal but was angry when her car was hit; on the swing boats where she did not want to stop; and on the big wheel where she wanted to stop at once and shrieked so that they had to slow it and take her down. She cried at Bingo when she did not win a prize and screamed when the mice ran into the ring in the mouse circus. Her father bought her a toffee apple which she licked once and threw away, a balloon which she burst, and a paper umbrella with which she hit at people's legs.

Having everything you want can make you very tired. When Clementina was tired she whined. "I don't like fairs," whined Clementina, "I want to go home." (Only she said, "I wa-ant to go ho-o-o-ome.")

"Come along then," said her father.

"Fetch the car," said Clementina, but motorcars cannot go into fairs; and, "I'm afraid you will have to walk," said her father.

Clementina was getting ready to cry when she heard a gay loud sound:

and a call, "Three f'r threepence! Seven f'r a tanner!" and she turned round and saw Candy Floss.

She saw Candy Floss sitting on Nuts, turning round and round as Nuts frisked up and down. Clementina saw the red shoes, the pink gauze, the way the blue eyes shone, the gold-spun hair, and, "I want that doll," said Clementina.

People often asked to buy Candy Floss, or Cocoa or Nuts; then Jack would laugh and say, "You'll have to buy me as well. We're pardners," and the people would laugh too, for they knew they could not buy Jack. "Candy Floss? Why, she's my luck, couldn't sell that," Jack would say. "Pretty as a pi'ture, ain't she?" said Jack.

Now Clementina's father came to Jack. "My little girl would like to buy your doll."

"Sorry, sir," said Jack. "Not f'r sale."

"I want her," said Clementina.

"I will give you a pound," said Clementina's father to Jack.

A pound is forty silver sixpences; but, "Not f'r five hundred pounds," said Jack.

"You see, Clementina," said her father.

"Give him five hundred pounds," said Clementina.

Her father walked away and Jack smiled at Clementina. "I said *not* f'r five hundred pounds, little missy."

I cannot tell you how furious was Clementina. She scowled at Jack (scowl means to make an ugly face). Jack stepped closer to Candy Floss and Cocoa growled; and, "You cut along to yer pa," said Jack to Clementina. Jack, of course, treated her as if she were any little girl, and she did not like that.

She made herself as tall as she could and said, "Do you know who I am? I am Clementina Davenport."

"And I'm Jack and these are Cocoa, Nuts, and Candy Floss," said Jack.

"I am Clementina Davenport," said Clementina scornfully. "I live in a big house. I have a room full of toys and a pony. I have a bicycle and twenty pairs of shoes."

"That's nice f'r you," said Jack, "but you can't have Candy Floss."

I believe that was the first time anyone had ever said "can't" to Clementina.

Jack thought he had settled it. In any case he was too busy picking up balls, taking in pennies and sixpences, handing out coconuts, and calling his call to pay much attention to Clementina. "Cut off," he told her, but Clementina did not cut off. She came nearer.

Cocoa, Nuts, and Candy Floss watched her out of the corners of their eyes.

Clementina was pretending not to be interested, but she came nearer still. If Candy Floss and Nuts had been breathing they would have held their breath.

Clementina came closer and at that moment Cocoa got down to take a lap of water from his bowl. (It was not

Cocoa's fault; he had never known a girl like Clementina.)

Nuts tried to turn faster, but he could only turn as fast as the music went. He wanted to kick, but he had to hold his forelegs up; he tried to shake his silver bells, but they did not make enough noise.

As Clementina's hand came out Candy Floss shrieked, "Help! Help!" but a doll's shriek has no sound. She tried to cling like a burr to the saddle, but she was too small.

When Jack turned round Candy Floss had gone. There was no sign of Clementina.

When Clementina snatched Candy Floss, quick-as-a-cat-can-wink-its-eye she hid her in the paper umbrella and ran after her father.

Candy Floss was head-downward, which made her dizzy. The umbrella banged against Clementina's legs as she ran and that gave Candy Floss great bumps. She trembled with terror as she felt herself being carried far away, perhaps. But she had not been brought up in a fair for nothing. She was used to being dizzy (on the merry-go-rounds), used to being bumped (on the bumper cars), used to trembling (on the big wheel), and when, in the big house on the hill, Clementina took her out of the umbrella Candy Floss looked almost as pretty and calm as she had on Nuts's saddle; but china can be cold and hard; she made herself cold and hard in Clementina's hands and her eyes looked as if they were the brightest, clearest glass.

Dolls cannot talk aloud; they talk in wishes. You and I have often felt them wish and we know how clear that can be, but Clementina had never played long enough with any of her dolls to feel a wish. She had never felt anything at all.

"But you will," said Candy Floss, "you will."

Clementina turned all her dolls'-house dolls out of the dolls' house, higgledy-piggledy onto the floor. "You will live in the dolls' house," she told Candy Floss.

"I live in a coconut shy," said Candy Floss and her dress caught on the prim little chairs and tables and her hair caught on the shells that edged the scrap-pictures. Every time Clementina moved her she upset something. When she had knocked down a lamp, spilled a vase of flowers, and pulled the cloth off a table, Clementina took her out.

"Don't live in the dolls' house then," said Clementina.

"You must wear another dress," said Clementina and tried to take the pink one off, but she did not know, as Jack knew, how to soften the glue. All she did was to tear the gauze. Then she tried to put another dress over the top of the gauze skirt, but it stuck out and Candy Floss made her arms so stiff they would not go in the sleeves.

Clementina lost patience and threw the dress on the floor.

She made a charming supper for Candy Floss: a daisy poached egg, some green grass spinach, and a blossom fruit salad with paint sauce. She had never taken such trouble over a supper before, but Candy Floss would not touch it.

"I eat hot dogs," said Candy Floss, "a chip, or a toffee apple." Nor would she take any notice of the dolls' house's best blue and white china. "I eat off a shell," said Candy Floss. "I drink from an acorn bowl."

"Eat it up," said Clementina, but Candy Floss tumbled slowly forward onto the supper and lay with her face in the blossom fruit salad.

"I shall put you to bed," scolded Clementina and she got out the dolls'-house bed.

"I don't sleep in a bed," said Candy Floss, "I sleep in a lolly drawer," and she made herself stiff so that her feet stuck out. When Clementina tucked them in, Candy Floss's head stuck out. Clementina put the bedclothes round her but they sprang up again at once. "Are you trying to fight me?" asked Clementina.

Candy Floss did not answer, but the bedclothes sprang up again.

"Well, you can sit on a chair all night," said Clementina and she took out a dolls'-house chair.

"I don't sit on a chair," said Candy Floss, "I sit on Nuts," and as soon as Clementina put her on the chair she fell off.

"*Sit!*" said Clementina in a terrible voice, but a doll brought up in the noise and shouts of a fair is not to be frightened by a little girl's voice and Candy Floss did not blink an eye. "Sit!" said Clementina and she sat Candy Floss hard on the chair. *Snap*, the chair legs broke.

Clementina stood looking at the pieces in her hand; she looked as if she were thinking. And if Candy Floss's little china mouth had not been smiling already, I should have said she smiled.

But she did not smile in the night. Clementina left her on the table when she went to bed and all night long Candy Floss lay on the cold table in that strange room.

There was no van; no music box with Nuts asleep under the old red cloth; no sound of Cocoa breathing; no Jack to feel big and warm; no lolly drawer to make a bed; no shamrock handkerchief. There was no music from the fair, no sixpence stars.

"And how can I get back?" asked Candy Floss. "I *can't* get back. Oh, how will the shy go on? What will Jack do without his luck?" And all night the frightening words beat in her head: "No luck. No luck. No Jack. No luck. No Nuts or Cocoa. No sixpences. No luck! No luck! No luck!"

Dolls cannot cry but they can feel. In the night Candy Floss felt so much she thought that she must crack.

Next morning it began again. Clementina took Candy
Floss into the garden. "You must go in my dolls'-house
perambulator," said Clementina.

"I go in a pocket," said Candy Floss, and she would
not fit in the perambulator. She held her head up so that
it would not go under the hood and made her legs stiff so
that they would not go in either. Clementina shook her
until her eyes came loose in her head.

"You belong to me now," said Clementina.

"I belong to Jack."

Candy Floss, as we know, could not say these things
aloud, but now Clementina was beginning to feel them.
Clementina was not used to feeling; the more she felt, the

angrier she grew, and she thought of something dreadful to say to Candy Floss. "Pooh!" said Clementina. "You're only a doll. The shops are full of dolls. Jack will have another doll by now. Do you think he wouldn't have bought another doll to take your place?"

Candy Floss seemed to sway in Clementina's hand. Another doll in her place! In all her places! On Nuts's back; in Jack's pocket; in the lolly drawer; in the shamrock handkerchief. Another doll to be Jack's luck! What shall I do? thought Candy Floss. What can I do? And she cried out with such a big wish that she fell out of Clementina's hand onto the path and a crack ran down her back. "Jack! Jack! Cocoa! Nuts! Help! Help! Help!" cried Candy Floss.

At that moment, in the fair, the merry-go-rounds started up.

All the merry-go-rounds up and down the heath began to play. The big wheel started and the rifles cracked in the rifle ranges. People began to cry "Bingo!" and the toy-sellers and balloon-sellers started to shout. All the music in the fair began to play, louder and louder, until it sounded as if the whole fair were in the garden.

Clementina picked Candy Floss up off the path, and what had happened? Candy Floss was cracked; her eyes were loose, the shine had gone out of her hair, her face was covered with paint where she had fallen into the salad, and her dress was torn. As for its pink, you know how brown and dull pink spun sugar can go. Candy Floss's dress looked just like that.

"You're horrid," said Clementina and she threw Candy Floss back onto the path.

The merry-go-round and the fair music seemed to say that too, "You're horrid", but they were saying it to Clementina.

"I think I shall go indoors and paint," said Clementina. She went in but the fair music came into the house and now, as Clementina listened, she heard other things as well. "She belongs to Jack." "You're horrid." "Cruel Clementina," said the music.

"I won't sit still. I shall skip," said Clementina, but though she skipped up to a hundred times she could not shut out that music. "She belongs to Jack." "Cruel Clementina." "Poor Candy Floss"; and the big wheel turning – you could see the top of it from the garden – seemed to say, "I can see. I see everything."

When lunchtime came Clementina did not want any lunch. "Are you ill?" asked her nurse and made Clementina lie down on her bed with a picture book. "You look quite bad," said the nurse.

"I don't!" shouted Clementina and hid under her blanket because that was what she did not want to feel, bad; but the bed and the picture book, even the blanket, could not shut out the fair, and the music never stopped:

"Bad Clementina." "Cruel Clementina." "She belongs to Jack." "Poor Candy Floss."

Clementina put her head under the pillow.

Under the pillow she could not hear the music but she heard something else: thumpity-bump; thumpity-bump; it was her own heart beating. Clementina had not known she had a heart before; now it thumped just like the merry-go-round engine, and what was it saying? "Poor Candy Floss. Poor Candy Floss," inside Clementina.

She lay very still. She was listening. Then she began to cry.

By and by Clementina sat up. She got out of bed and put on her shoes; then, just as she was, rumpled and crumpled from lying on the bed and tear-stained from crying, she tiptoed out of the room and went down the stairs into the garden, where she picked up Candy Floss and tiptoed to the gate.

No one was about. She opened the gate and ran.

She ran up the hill to the heath and into the fair, past the balloon-man and the toy-sellers, the fish-and-chips bar, the hot-dog stands and the toffee-apple stalls. She ran past the little merry-go-rounds with the buses and cars, and the big merry-go-rounds with the horses and swans, past the Bingos, the mouse circus, the rifle ranges, and the big wheel . . . and then she stopped.

The coconut shy was closed.

No lights shone; no coconuts were set up on the red

and white posts. The balls were stacked in their scarlet stands. The music box was covered with the old red cloth. Nuts could not be seen. Cocoa lay on the ground with his head on his paws; now and again he whimpered.

Jack was sitting on a box, hunched and still. When people came to the shy he shook his head. "My luck's gone," he said, and Cocoa put up his nose and howled.

Clementina had meant to put Candy Floss back on Nuts and then run away as fast as she could, but she could not bear it when she saw how miserable she had made them all. She could not bear to see Nuts covered up, Cocoa whimpering, Jack's sad face; and, without thinking or waiting, she cried, "Oh *please*, don't be so sorry! I have brought her back."

Jack stood up. Cocoa stood up. The cloth slithered off the music box and there was Nuts, standing up. "Brought her *back*?" asked Jack, and Clementina forgot all about being Clementina Davenport in the big house on the hill; and, "Yes, I'm Clementina. I took her," she said and burst into tears.

When Jack saw what Clementina had done to Candy Floss he looked very, very grave and Cocoa growled; but Jack was used to mending things and in no time at all he had borrowed some china cement from the china-smashing stall and filled in the crack. He would not let Clementina hold Candy Floss but he let her watch, though Cocoa still growled softly under his breath. Very gently he touched the loosened eyes with glue and made them firm again. He washed the torn skirt off and glued a fresh one on and cleaned the paint off Candy Floss's face; then he spun out her hair again and she looked as good as new. Cocoa stopped growling and Clementina actually smiled.

Then in a jiffy (which was what Jack called a moment) he put fresh coconuts on the posts and opened the ball stands. He put Cocoa's bow on and told him to jump up on the stool; he ran over Nuts's paint with a rag so that it shone; then he put Candy Floss in the saddle and switched on the music box.

went the music box.

"Three balls f'r threepence! Seven f'r a tanner!" called Jack. His shout sounded so joyful, Cocoa begged so cleverly, Nuts frisked so happily, and Candy Floss turned so gaily that the crowds flocked to the shy. "Come'n help!" called Jack to Clementina and Clementina began to pick up the balls.

But who was this coming? It was Clementina's father and mother and with them the nurse and all the maids and a policeman, because there had been *such* a fuss when they had missed Clementina. They had searched all through the fair. Now they stopped at the coconut shy.

"Is *that* Clementina?" asked her father and mother, the nurse and the maids.

The cross look had gone from Clementina's face; she was too busy to be cross. Her cheeks were as pink as Candy Floss's dress; her eyes were shining as if they were made of glass; her hair looked almost gold.

"*Can* it be Clementina?" asked her father and mother, the nurse and the maids.

"Clementina, Clementina!" they called, amazed.

"Three f'r threepence! Seven f'r a tanner!" yelled Clementina.

"What *am* I to do with her?" cried her mother.

It was the policeman who answered, the policeman who had been called out to look for Clementina. "If I was you, mum," said the policeman. "I should leave her alone."

Clementina was allowed to stay all afternoon at the shy. Her father and mother thought it was they who allowed her; Jack thought it was Jack. She worked so hard picking up balls that he gave her two sixpences for herself, and Clementina was prouder of those sixpences than of all the pound notes in her money box (she calls it a lolly box now). "I *earned* them," said Clementina.

When her nurse came to take her home she had to say good-bye to Jack, Cocoa, Nuts, and Candy Floss; but,

"Not good-bye, so long," said Jack.

"So long?" asked Clementina.

"So long as there's fairs we'll be back," said Jack. "Come'n look f'r us."

When Clementina was in bed and happily asleep the fair went on.

went the music box.

"Three f'r threepence! Seven f'r a tanner!" called Jack. Cocoa begged, Nuts frisked, and Candy Floss went round and round.